"I'd like to kiss the bride."

She recovered from her surprise quickly. "I expect it to be part of the ceremony."

"I mean, let's do it now."

"What?"

"Molly," Adam said, urgency rising from his core. "I don't want our first kiss to be in front of an audience. Even a small select audience. It wouldn't—it won't be right. Besides, it will take the pressure off the actual moment, right?"

Molly stilled. "Well—all right."

Adam stepped over to his best friend—his bride-to-be. He lifted his hands and brushed her hair off her shoulders.

He'd dated a lot of women, kissed the majority of them, at the very least. But he hadn't had any idea that he compared any of them to Molly until this moment, when she stood before him. And that's when he knew—he was in big, big trouble.

Dear Reader,

In writing ***A Little Change Of Plans,*** I had to throw the hero and the heroine for a big loop. They thought they had their futures figured out long ago.

Uh-huh. Well, life may be about a lot of things, but I don't think it's ever about certainty.

As soon as I met Molly and Adam, I decided they would each have to let go of their illusion of what they thought they always wanted if they were to find real and lasting love and happiness. (And because *I'm* their author, what I say goes!)

I really hope these characters inspire you the way they inspired me, to live with an open heart and embrace all the surprising possibilities that inevitably appear.

All the best,

Jen Safrey

A LITTLE CHANGE OF PLANS

JEN SAFREY

Silhouette®
SPECIAL EDITION®
Published by Silhouette Books
America's Publisher of Contemporary Romance

Special thanks and acknowledgment are given
to Jen Safrey for her contribution to the
TALK OF THE NEIGHBORHOOD miniseries.

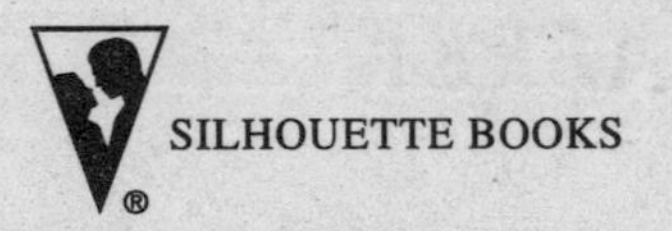

ISBN-13: 978-0-373-24780-6
ISBN-10: 0-373-24780-X

A LITTLE CHANGE OF PLANS

This edition published by arrangement with Harlequin Books S.A.

Visit Silhouette Books at www.eHarlequin.com

Printed in U.S.A.

Books by Jen Safrey

Silhouette Special Edition

A Perfect Pair #1590
Ticket to Love #1697
Secrets of a Good Girl #1719
A Little Change of Plans #1780

JEN SAFREY

is a back-to-back recipient of the 2004 and 2005 Golden Leaf Awards for Long Contemporary Romance. She's steadily moving up the belt ranks in tae kwon do, although her back kicks still need some work. She's also learning to cook (finally), so feel free to e-mail her your recipes—easy ones—through her Web site at www.jensafreybooks.com.

Motherhood is a path I chose not to travel,
so this book is dedicated to the brave women
in my life who did, and shared their adventures with
me—particularly my sister, Elizabeth Markman,
and, of course, my own terrific mom.

Prologue

June 1992

"Molly, you have been an asset to Saint Cecilia's Girls' Academy. I guess this is the last time I'll meet with you as your guidance counselor."

Molly crossed her legs at the ankle and straightened her spine. Ms. Glass regarded her, and Molly basked in the pride reflected through the woman's thick glasses.

"Now," the administrator continued, "I know I don't have to ask you if you've given serious thought to what you want to study next year. I have a little feeling you've been mulling it over since you were in pigtails."

"I'm going to earn a bachelor's degree, then an MBA, and then start my own business," Molly said with a smile.

The smile was returned by the older woman, but in it Molly detected a jaded tinge.

Molly didn't take it personally. She imagined plenty of Saint Cecilia's alumni returned every year with careers and lives miles and miles off the fast track, so far from what they'd once envisioned for themselves at this elite private school.

She, Molly Jackson, would not be among them. When she returned—if, of course, she had time to make the trip back to California from New York between power lunches and business-class trips to Europe—she would be feted as a success, maybe even with a scholarship founded in her name....

"Remember your first day as a freshman, Molly?" Ms. Glass asked, interrupting her reverie. "When I first met you? You walked into this office wearing a lovely, smart pink blazer. The rest of the girls were in jeans."

Molly nodded, not really recalling her wardrobe that particular day and now wondering what the point of this discussion was going to be.

"You marched in here, sat down in that same chair there, and said, 'I'm going to earn my bachelor's, then an MBA, then start my own business.'"

Molly waited. She probably did say that.

"You were so sure of yourself then," Ms. Glass continued, "and even more sure of yourself now."

"Excuse me," Molly said, frowning, "but it sounds like you think that's a bad thing."

"It's a wonderful thing," Ms. Glass said. "I have no doubt you'll go wherever you want to go and do whatever you want to do. But I give every student of mine a piece of advice to take into the real world, and here's yours: Let life just happen to you once in a while, Molly."

Molly pulled her chin in, taken aback.

"Things are different after high school," Ms. Glass went on. "Life may not turn out the way you expect, and you need to be able to adjust, relax, go with the flow."

Molly raised an eyebrow. "This sounds like the opposite of normal guidance counselor advice."

"Normal guidance counselor advice has never been something you really needed, Molly. I'm giving you woman-to-woman advice. Be spontaneous at least once in a while. Maybe once a year? Have fun. Meet boys."

Molly *had* given boys some thought over the last few years, and she didn't want to tell Ms. Glass that it happened to be another area in which she was quite sure of herself and of what would happen.

Out there was a boy just like herself.

A boy who worked hard, who put achieving first. A boy whose parents taught him how to strive to be the best. A boy who participated in student government, band, mathletes and excelled in a varsity sport. Maybe track and field.

Molly was going to find that boy, the one who was destined to be the man for her. A driven, ambitious man, exactly like the woman she was about to be.

She'd find him, and he wouldn't be hard to find. They'd be drawn to one another without effort, ready and able to support one another, work side by side forever in perfect synchronized partnership.

College started in three months. He could be anywhere.

Molly stood, smoothed out the wrinkles in her black pants the way she knew her mother did and put out her hand. "Thank you for everything, Ms. Glass. I'm proud to have attended this school, and I promise, I won't let Saint Cecilia's down."

"Don't worry about us," Ms. Glass said, clasping Molly's hand and looking deep into her eyes. "Just think about yourself. And be happy."

June 1992

"Well, Adam, it's that time for you. This will be our last meeting."

"Yup."

"So, I beg you, please tell me you've decided what you plan to study next year."

Adam leaned back and eyed Mr. Fisher. His guidance counselor stared back at him with a stern expression that Adam was certain had to have been a course requirement for the man to earn his education degree. The thought of a roomful of men and women staring each other down, practicing and perfecting their faces for the final exam, made Adam grin.

"I'm glad you're so unconcerned and amused," Mr. Fisher said, sitting back in his chair and lacing his fingers together on the blotter in front of him. "I wouldn't want you to be losing sleep over your unclear future."

"I'm not, Mr. F.," Adam said, pretending he didn't understand the sarcasm so as not to prolong the argument.

Adam didn't take it personally. It was Mr. Fisher's job to make sure his students didn't return to Grover Cleveland High School year after year and tell him about their miserable rat-race lives of drudgery and nine-to-five-plus-overtime.

He, Adam Shibbs, would not be among them. When he returned—if he had time between checking out jazz clubs, discovering Middle Eastern restaurants and getting the local guys together to shoot hoops—he would have an easy smile on his face, a man happy with life and free to sample all the world had to offer.

"I know you've had a very difficult year," Mr. Fisher said after a pause. His voice and face softened. "Losing a parent is a terrible experience."

Adam, his levity fading away, looked down at the

dusty floor, and wondered what the point of this discussion would be.

"But I don't want to see you permanently stunt your growth as a person, Adam," Mr. Fisher said. "Your grades are pretty good for an average student, but for a boy as bright as you, they're a definite underachievement. Still, they were enough to get you into a good college, and my advice to you is to consider buckling down for a few years. Get motivated. See what your brain can do."

"I use my brain," Adam said. "I just don't use it in the way you think I should. I don't use it thinking of ways to get ahead and be great at everything, and earn a million dollars a year and make mergers and whatever else. I use it to try to learn about things that amaze me or make me laugh, so I can have a good time." He paused. "You only live once."

"I agree," his guidance counselor said. "And sometimes, as I know you learned the hard way, your one life can throw you a lot of curveballs. You've got to know how to hit them, even if you don't want or expect them to come at you. You coped this time around by easing up and relaxing, and that was fine, but maybe now it's time to work hard for a while. Find your potential. Prepare yourself to face anything in the real world, and to meet anyone."

Adam didn't want to admit it, but he *had* been giving the part about meeting people a lot of thought.

Out there were many women just like himself—

fun, carefree, exciting, adventurous. He planned to meet as many women as was possible and enjoy the wide, beautiful variety the world had to offer. And if he ever got to the point where it was time to settle down—although he couldn't imagine that, really—he'd be acquainted with many to choose from. Women who didn't work themselves to death, so that he wouldn't have to love and lose someone again.

Women exactly like him. It was a huge planet. They wouldn't be hard to find.

College started in three months. They could be everywhere.

Adam bent to retie the tattered lace on his sneaker, then stood and put out his hand. "Thanks for everything, Mr. Fisher. I did have fun most of the time here at G.C. High. I promise I'll be fine."

"Don't promise me anything," Mr. Fisher said, clasping his hand. "You're the one with the promise. Just don't ignore it."

Chapter One

Molly Jackson's pros/cons for keeping her birthday to herself—

Pros:

1. Don't have to laugh weakly at lame jokes that go, "Let me guess. twenty-nine again, right?" Thirty-two is not only chronologically correct but absolutely acceptable.
2. Don't have to worry about getting dragged out to a bar or restaurant by well-meaning Danbury Way women only to quietly obsess for three hours that I could be at home preparing

that report for my newest client and worry that I'm wasting valuable time.
3. Don't have to deflect curious, endless questions about my getting-bigger stomach. Don't have to smile distantly and nod vaguely when the words "sperm bank" inevitably come up. Don't have to feel guilty, and then extra guilty that I feel guilty.
4. Staying indoors all day means my hair won't frizz up in the rain.

Cons:
1. Have to make my own cake.

The rain splattered down harder, startling Molly from her thoughts for a moment, but as she watched water stream down the windowpane, she was pulled back into the haven of her organized mind.

Molly was never off task for long, whatever the task happened to be.

Ten minutes later, she was con-less and convinced she'd made the right gut decision about her birthday. Plus, she was itching to get in to her office to start plowing through her in-box. She glanced up at the kitchen clock, which she could see from where she sprawled in the center of her soft, bouncy sofa—8:00 a.m. on the dot. She rose—or tried to rise. Her new weight unbalanced her and she fell back down, her behind sinking into the crevice between the sofa cushions. She was surprised it fit in there, because lately, she'd noticed her back end widening inch by inch, minute by minute. At this rate, by next week she'd be turning sideways to go through doorways. Someone would have to slap a Wide Load sign on the butt of her heather-gray sweatpants, the only item of clothing in her closet that she could still breathe in.

In what was becoming a common occurrence, her noncuddly, nonmaternal thoughts dissolved into guilt. "Sorry, baby," she said, patting her stomach gently. "I'm just not used to you being so—so there." She sighed. "Every day, you take me as much by surprise as the day I found out about you."

Thinking about that, and thinking about how every day for the rest of her life would contain a persistent element of unexpectedness, Molly felt love. And hiding just underneath that thick cozy cover of love, a thinner, shakier stranger of a feeling that could possibly be—

No. Not fear. Molly refused fear. Never let it in.

She planted both palms on the couch and hurled herself up so efficiently she almost flew across the room into the wall. She walked to the staircase and ascended it, each deliberate step taking her away from the moment where she might have given in to her feelings, admitted what the fear did to her, welcomed this emotion she so rarely experienced.

And she refused to experience it, to surrender to it now. She was a single, pregnant career woman, and she couldn't afford to give in to—that emotion.

She pushed through the door to her office and sat down. She glanced around at the clutterless desk, the efficient file cabinet, the dust-free computer monitor. This was control. She was in control. She could do anything she put her determined mind to.

The phone rang, and she donned her headset. She switched her computer on with one hand as she clicked onto the phone line with her other hand. "M.J. Consulting," she said, her tone crisp.

She smiled, the same way she did after answering every first phone call of the day. She so loved the name of her own one-woman company. She particularly loved the name of her own company spoken by her in her own office, in her very own still-felt-like-new home.

"Yes, Mr. Trent, how are you?" she asked, leaving the smile on her face so it would come through the receiver on her client's end. She reached for a pen out of her pencil cup and her hand came up a half-inch short.

Listening intently, Molly leaned forward. She tried not to groan into her headset as her stomach pressed against the desk, holding her back, keeping her capable fingertips just out of reach.

Busy, busy, busy all day long and that was just fine with Molly. By a quarter to four, she was famished, even after having eaten a massive roast-beef sandwich just a few hours ago. She stretched her arms over her head and contracted her tight lower back. Through the narrow break between the filmy lilac-colored curtains, she spied Sylvia Fulton walking back from her mailbox with a pile of magazines and catalogs, a filmy pink scarf tied over her gray hair. Molly waved one of her hands over her head and, squinting, Sylvia waved back, even though she probably couldn't see Molly, just the shadowy motion of her greeting.

Molly got up and rubbed her lower back. Getting the mail was a good excuse to get blood circulating in her legs again.

She went downstairs and grabbed her umbrella from the pail beside the front door. It was only about twelve paces to the mailbox, but she might as well try to minimize the inevitable hair frizz.

The wind sent a spray of rain into her face, so she tilted her umbrella in front of her—which was why she didn't see Irene Dare and Rhonda Johnson loitering in front of her house until it was too late to ignore them.

"Hi," Molly said neutrally, sliding her unimportant-after-all mail from her box and turning to go.

"Molly!" Irene said. "You look just wonderful."

"Wonderful," Rhonda echoed.

Molly laid a hand on her stomach and silently apologized to her baby for exposing it to the nasty elements so early in its development. And she wasn't thinking about the weather.

Rhonda smiled at Molly from under a bright blue umbrella, Irene from a light pink one. Despite the miniature terriers each woman carried like infants, their two smiles reminded Molly of the sly Siamese cats in *Lady and the Tramp.*

"I was just saying to Irene as we passed your house, 'I wonder how Molly's doing,'" Rhonda purred—er, said. "And I said, 'She's so brave.'"

"Not that brave," Molly said. "It's probably safe to assume that women have been having babies since the dawn of humanity."

"I mean, brave for doing it without a man around to help you."

"Oh, I don't think a man will be able to push better than I can when the big day comes."

Undaunted, Irene chimed in, "You know, there are some people who say that going to a sperm bank is, well, desperate. But *I* don't agree with that at all."

"No?" Molly asked, echoing the sarcasm.

"No, of course not," Irene went on. "In fact, if I were in your shoes— What I mean is, just getting to the age where it was time to finally give up on finding a man and have a baby on my own—it might be nice to be able to pick and choose what sperm I wanted. Custom-built baby." She grinned.

"Irene? A baby?" Molly heard someone say, and all three women turned to find Rebecca Peters had walked two doors down from her place. "First of all, one can only assume you're speaking theoretically."

Irene, who Molly knew full well was obsessive about preserving her gym-toned looks, sputtered at the not-so-subtle insult.

"Besides," Rebecca went on smoothly, "would you really be able to handle one more *big* mouth to feed?"

The grin flew off Rhonda's face and landed on Molly's. She covered it discreetly with her hand.

"Rebecca, how lovely to see you," Rhonda said. "Too bad we were just leaving." They turned their backs, but before they walked away, Rhonda said over her shoulder, "Molly, you should run inside now if you want to save your hair. Although it looks like it might be too late."

Rebecca put two fingers in her mouth and made a vomiting sound. "Those two rats. And I'm not even talking about their scrawny little dogs." She laid a hand on Molly's shoulder. "I saw them waylay you from my window, so I figured I'd come to your rescue before your hormones made you do something you'd regret."

Molly reached up and squeezed Rebecca's long, graceful fingers. "Thank you. Although I'm not sure I would have ever regretted it."

"Good point." Rebecca's sharp blue eyes flashed with leftover rebellion. "I seriously can't believe their nerve. You know, people insist the city is cold and rude. But let me tell you, I never had to deal with anyone like that before I moved to quiet little Danbury Way."

"Please don't let them spoil Rosewood for you," Molly said. "No one else is like them, you know that."

"Yeah, I think I do."

"Besides, they live around the corner on Maplewood. They're not Danbury Way-ers."

The two women surveyed the wet street companionably from their dead end of the cul-de-sac. Now that Irene and Rhonda had slunk off, they were the only ones out in the dismal weather. After a few moments, Rebecca turned around. "It's hysterical how from this spot, our places look like little outhouses for Carly's mega-mansion."

Molly giggled. As much as she loved her home, and as nice as the house was that Rebecca was renting, they unfortunately flanked the ostentatious brick edifice.

"Good thing I adore Carly so much," Rebecca said, "or I might be jealous."

"No, I think if I was going to bother being jealous, it would be of that new man of hers."

Rebecca grinned. "Yeah, Bo's something else. I'm happy for them. Listen, you'd better get back inside. You don't want to catch a cold."

"I'm fine. But it's my hair, isn't it?"

"Oh, you're gorgeous and you know it."

"And for that, you're invited for lunch tomorrow."

"Cool. I'll come by around noon." She turned to go.

"Rebecca."

She swiveled back around. "Yeah?"

"Thanks."

Her friend waved it off. "Please. Don't you know we city girls are always looking for a fight?" She put up her fists and gave a one-two punch to the air in front of her.

Molly laughed. Rebecca waggled her fingers on both hands, then jogged by Carly's massive lawn and disappeared around the back of the house.

Molly's smile lingered even on her getting-harder-every-time climb up the stairs back to her office. She was glad to be getting closer to Rebecca, who worked for a fashion magazine and had a lot of Molly's own ambition and drive. She wondered what Rebecca would say if she knew the truth about the baby's father. She had a strong feeling that she could trust Rebecca to keep it to herself, and that she wouldn't judge Molly, but even still, Molly was too ashamed to say it out loud to anyone, to hear herself admit the facts.

Even her own parents back in California assumed she went to a sperm bank. It didn't surprise them in the least. They were used to their daughter doing things the unconventional way—buying her own house, starting her own business. They were also used to their daughter's success—being as they had such an influence on instilling it in the first place—so they had no doubts about Molly's decisions. They stood behind her, but at a distance. Just like they always did.

The person who'd stood closest to her for so long

was Adam, her unlikely best friend. He didn't know anything about the baby, either. She hadn't seen him since the reunion, where, preoccupied, she'd inadvertently left without saying goodbye. They'd only exchanged a few innocuous "hi, how are you? I'm still alive" e-mails since then. Molly didn't question Adam's lying low because she was too busy doing it herself. She'd tell him she was pregnant the next time they really talked, but she didn't imagine she could bring herself to tell even him the truth.

Molly's stomach growled, and when she scowled down at it, she saw the baby move. It was bad enough she ate more in a day than she did in a week prepregnancy, without her own body and the extra person occupying it rebelling against her.

She contemplated what was left in her kitchen, and after a minute or so, the phone rang again.

"I'll make this quick, baby," Molly said to her middle. "Then I'll feed us."

It was Friday afternoon, and she was anticipating a weekend of planning her eventual spring garden. Today she'd lined all her business ducks up in a harmoniously quacking row for next week. Whatever this was, it couldn't set her too far back.

"M.J. Consulting," she said, smiling again.

Less than two minutes later, her smile was gone.

Chapter Two

Adam propped his feet up on his second-floor balcony railing, and watched the rain drip onto his bare toes. He'd been planning since yesterday to pick up pad thai on the way home from work today and eat dinner al fresco. September 1 meant summer was on its way out, and he wanted to breathe in the warm air as long as it still surrounded him. Winter in upstate New York had its different snow-covered enjoyments, but it wasn't time for that just yet.

So with these ambitious plans—and with Adam, this was as ambitious as it got—a day-long deluge wouldn't change anything. The overhang from his upstairs neighbor's balcony kept his head and his dinner dry. A few raindrops on his ankles were no hardship.

A tiny black furry flash tore out of the half-open sliding glass door and slid with a soft thud into the wall under Adam's feet. Just barely righting himself, the Labrador puppy then collided into Adam's chair leg, and jumped once to try to see what was in his owner's dish. Then he bumped himself into the wall again, and ran back to Adam again, panting with the excitement of trying to figure out where the most fun was at that moment.

"Elmer," Adam said. Elmer quivered, looking at Adam's face, his hands, his dish, his feet. Adam chuckled. Elmer didn't know his own name, but his exuberance at just hearing Adam's voice was gratifying.

Adam hoped someone else would be just as happy to hear his voice, as soon as he got around to calling her to wish her a happy birthday. He wasn't putting it off or anything. It wasn't even dark yet. Technically, Molly's birthday didn't end until midnight.

Waiting until the absolute last minute would be kind of cheesy.

Well, they hadn't talked to each other at all for approximately six months. She could certainly wait fifteen more minutes while he finished his pad thai. He put a forkful into his mouth. Elmer miniyelped and wagged his tail, watching Adam chew.

Besides, if Molly was so distressed at the six-month hiatus from his voice, she could just as well have picked up the phone and called him.

He shook his head at himself and took a long swallow of ginger ale. The truth was, a six-month hiatus wasn't exactly unusual in their friendship. Even in college, living in the same dorm, they both knew—verbal acknowledgment unnecessary—that they couldn't spend many consecutive hours in each other's presence. Adam's laid-back attitude got on Molly's impatient nerves, and Molly's constant running around gave Adam a serious case of motion sickness. Still, despite their obvious limitations, they each bestowed upon the other the title of best friend. For Adam—and he guessed for Molly, too—no one else had ever seemed to qualify for the position, and at some point soon after they met, the job was filled and no other applicants were considered.

After college, they'd gone their own separate ways, and drifted in and out of each other's everyday lives. Some weeks, they chatted on the phone nightly. And sometimes months went by without an exchanged word or e-mail. The thing was, Adam always knew she was there, and that was enough. More than that was neediness, which sounded like a relationship, which was synonymous with trouble, as far as he was concerned.

The past six months were different, though, in that Adam had deliberately stayed away. The last time he'd seen her, she was leaving their ten-year college reunion with her long-unrequited crush, Zach Jones. Not just leaving with him, but leaving with his arm possessively around her waist, laughing up at him, her head thrown back so far her dark curls brushed the alluring curve of her behind.

Adam could have called her anytime after that. He could have said, "So. Zach Jones. You finally bagged that creep." And she could have said, "Why do you care?" And maybe that's why he'd never called—because he didn't have an answer to that particular question for her. Or for himself.

She also could have said, "He turned out to be a jerk, just like you always thought." And maybe that was one more reason he'd never called—because he didn't want to give her the opportunity to *not* say that.

Whatever. Molly had a right to leave a party with anyone she wanted, even a schmuck like Zach Jones. And Adam had a right not to talk to her about it. So he'd limited his contact to a few random, somewhat impersonal e-mails—and her responses weren't more than acknowledgments. Maybe she was avoiding him, too?

He shoveled in another mouthful of pad thai, slightly colder than the last bite. Elmer turned his puppy face up to the dark clouds in the distance and a stray raindrop blew into his eye. He blinked and shook and yelped again, wagging his happy tail.

The thing was, Molly had no idea Adam's silence was anything but golden. She had no idea how inexplicably annoyed he was with her, with her uncharacteristically poor judgment. But if he failed to call her on her birthday, that was an egregious error. One that she would remember and hold over his head. That part, he could handle. But she'd be hurt, too, and that part he couldn't handle. Hurting a woman like Molly Jackson by not calling her on her birthday would make *him* the schmuck.

Another bite of dinner was the deciding factor. "I think this is destined for the microwave, buddy," he said, standing. Elmer leaped as high as he could, barely scraping Adam's kneecap.

"Down, boy. I meant for tomorrow," Adam said. "For lunch." He stepped into his living room and Elmer trotted in behind him. Adam slid the door shut. "I have to make a call," he continued, heading into the kitchen and reaching under the sink for the aluminum foil. "I have to wish Molly a happy birthday. I don't know what else we're going to talk about, but I know one thing is for sure." He tore off a piece of foil, fitted it over the dinner plate and slid it into the refrigerator. "It'll probably be a more interesting and complex conversation than these deep ones I have with you. No offense."

Elmer wagged his tail, eyeballing the bottom shelf of the open refrigerator. Adam closed the door.

"You and I have fun, though, huh?" He rubbed his dog's head. "Molly. Now that's a girl who's not about fun. She's about work. Maybe she thinks work *is* fun."

Elmer groaned and lay down on the linoleum.

"I agree. She's nuts. People like that—" An image of his father floated to the front of his memory. Dad, who always did everything one-handed because the other hand was always clutching either a phone or a legal pad or his briefcase. "People like that—they die way too early," Adam finished weakly. "They're not for us."

Elmer stared at him, uncomprehending.

"Molly is—well, Molly just needs to get out more," Adam said.

Remembering that the last time he saw Molly she *was* going out and then he held it against her, he felt bad enough to finally grab the phone off the charger and dial her number. Before he got to the last digit, he hung up and tried to decide how he was going to musically deliver the happy birthday message. Traditional version? Beatles version? Finally deciding on the smelling-like-a-monkey version—even though he suspected he might have done that one last year—he redialed Molly's number.

"Hello?"

Something was wrong. Molly's voice was muffled, like she was speaking into the wrong end of a megaphone, or she was underwater, or she was…crying?

Molly? Crying?

"Molly?"

He was answered with a big, wet sniffle.

"I wouldn't have pegged you for the birthday blues," he ventured.

No answer yet, but was that a sob? Sounded like a strangled something in the back of her throat.

Worried, Adam tried again with humor. "Come on, Moll, maybe you're over the hill but you're not totally decrepit yet. You looked pretty good the last time I saw you." In that short black dress and illegally high heels, she'd looked better than pretty good, in fact. And he hadn't been the only one who'd thought so.

"Thirty-two is not over the hill, Shibbs," she finally said, petulance obvious even under the sniffling.

"Sure it is. It's all downhill from here."

"I'm not in the mood for jokes right now."

That wasn't what worried Adam, because Molly wasn't exactly someone aligned to Adam's constant levity. It was the tears that were concerning. "Come on. Didn't your birthday wishes come true?"

"Actually, let me think," she said, sniffling so hard she coughed twice. "You know, I guess they did come true after all. This morning I woke up and thought, 'Oh, it's my birthday. I think the best gift anyone can give me today is a nice big stack of walking papers!' And I had to wait the whole day, but just as I was finishing up work, at the very last second, I got my wish!"

Adam's mouth hung open, and he thought it was very possible he was just as surprised as Molly must have been. "You got fired?"

"Only by my biggest client. No big deal." She sighed, and a little sob came out with it.

"I'm sorry. That's terrible."

"I never got fired before."

Neither had Adam, but he considered it best to keep that to himself. Molly was well aware of his relaxed work style, and it wasn't going to make her feel any better that she'd now been canned one more time than he had.

"What happened?"

"Nothing happened. It wasn't me. It was budget cuts. They had to let a lot of people go. An outside consultant wasn't someone they were willing to save at the expense of one of their full-timers."

"Of course not."

"I begged them to keep me. I told them I'd revise our plans, make it more affordable, anything. It was humiliating, the way I acted. It was even worse than the firing part."

"Then why did you?"

"I'm losing a big chunk of income."

"Listen, it wasn't your fault."

"Well, I can't exactly write 'Not my fault' on my mortgage check."

"No, but your business has been going well enough to land you that gig in the first place. M.J. Consulting has a great rep. You'll get another job soon enough. And you've got other clients. So you'll eat mac-and-cheese and Ramen noodles for a couple of weeks, and by then you'll have recovered. Tighten your belt a little."

"Trust me, that's not even physically possible."

"What do you mean?"

She sighed again, and this time it wasn't accompanied by sobs and sniffles. Just noisy mouth breathing, caused by her now certainly stuffed nose.

"You know, I've been asking you for years to breathe heavy for me on the phone, babe, but you refused," he joked.

"We can't eat Ramen for weeks," Molly said flatly.

"Sure you can. I can teach you 750 ways to cook that stuff—" Wait a minute. We? "We?" he asked. Was Zach Jones—there? Sitting next to her while she had this conversation? And if he was, why wasn't he the one reassuring her, comforting her, trying to make her smile?

"Yeah. We. There's two of us now, Adam. I haven't—I suppose we haven't talked in a while."

"Well, I guess I should have known when you left with Jones at the reunion."

She sputtered. "What? What do you take me for?"

"Just a woman who's in love with a jerk." Adam cringed. That just slipped out. He couldn't help it. "Just tell him if he loves you, mac-and-cheese shouldn't be a problem."

"Oh, my God, Adam," Molly said slowly. "If I didn't know for a fact you're smart, I'd call you an idiot. Zach's not *here.* He dumped me when that weekend was barely over."

"Molly, I'm—"

"Adam, I'm pregnant. It's Zach's."

Adam opened his mouth, closed it, opened it again, and found he couldn't stop doing it.

"I can't believe I told you that. Actually, I'm glad I did," Molly amended. "I'm sick of keeping it to myself. No one knows."

"About the baby?"

"Well, it's kind of hard to hide a baby when you're six months pregnant. No one knows about where the baby came from. Everyone around here, all my neighbors and friends, sort of quietly assumed I went to a sperm bank."

"And you sort of quietly didn't correct them."

"What's your point?"

"No point. Getting it all straight." So Molly, my-life-is-a-well-oiled-machine Molly, was single, pregnant and financially shaky. That would be all of it straight.

"So you were right," Molly said. "Zach is a jerk."

For some reason, Adam was missing the deep satisfaction he'd expected to have upon hopefully hearing those words.

"So," Adam said, "what's your plan for this? Molly Jackson has an answer to everything."

A long pause. "I know. But my best answer is far from a sure thing."

"What's the plan?"

"Well, there's this Dutch chemical company called ALCOP that's ready to open up a big plant here in Rosewood in a couple of weeks. They're looking for a consultant to implement their human resources needs."

"That's right up your alley."

"I've got great experience, sterling references—including the firm who just fired me, by the way, because they actually did like me—and I know I'd be the best local person this chem company can find. And it will be about six times the size of any other firm I've done work for. It's a yearlong commitment, so I can count on the money being good for at least that long."

"What's not the sure thing?"

"Well, see, I heard about ALCOP not too long ago, and I decided then not to go for it. I had that other big client and besides, I've heard that the company president, Pieter Tilberg, is notorious for not hiring women for key positions."

"Isn't that illegal?"

"Illegal or not, the glass ceiling hangs in too many places to count. That's the way it is. That's part of the reason why I struck out on my own in the first place."

"You are woman. I hear you roaring."

"Funny, Shibbs. So I figured, I'm doing fine, I don't have the time, and besides, if this ALCOP guy's got an issue with women, I can only imagine the issues he'd have with a single, pregnant one. But now—"

"Now you've got to take that chance?"

"I got fired at four o'clock. And I've now spent about five hours putting together a proposal," she said. "And you know what? It's flawless. Anyone would hire me. Even *I* would hire me. But when I walk in there, Tilberg won't see my brain. He'll see my big belly. And he won't want to see it again. I'll lose this chance, not because of my résumé but because of my private life."

She broke down again, sobbing hard. "I've hardly even *had* a private life," she managed to add.

Adam's mind raced to take Molly-like control. "All right. You have to calm down. Freaking out is not useful. It's not on the to-do list."

Molly, a historical fan of lists, ceased her sobs a bit. When he could count to at least five between them, Adam said, "Did you get yourself an interview?"

"At the very last second," Molly said shakily. "By the time I pulled myself together and made my decision, it was nearly six o'clock. I think I caught the HR director as she was leaving for the day. I hope I didn't sound too desperate."

"You're not desperate."

"The hell I'm not."

"You're not. Desperate people are people without resources. You have plenty of those. You have your brains, your résumé, your references…and me."

"Oh, you, huh? You work for Gibraltar Foods, which has nothing to do with what I do. And besides, you don't even care about work. You're not much help to me right now. No offense."

"Listen," he said, "you're a woman, and although

in this day and age you could certainly change that, you don't want to. And you're pregnant, and that's not changing, either. But one element of your situation is changeable, flexible. Masqueradeable."

"I have no idea what the hell you're talking about."

"I'm talking about your being single. Why does anyone have to know that? Just during your big meeting, casually mention your devoted husband, Adam Shibbs."

"What?" She pitched the word so high, she sounded like one of Alvin and the Chipmunks.

"Just tell the chem company honcho that you happen to be married. I'll give you a ride from the interview and you can say your husband's picking you up."

"Adam, that's not going to work. I appreciate the innovation behind the idea, but this place will undoubtedly do a background check. Then not only will I be exposed as single, but a big old liar on top of that."

Adam blew a breath out from his bottom lip, and he felt the air on the tip of his nose. "So get married."

Molly laughed an unamused, sharp laugh. "Oh, sure, no problem. Let me just run out right now and grab a man off the street."

"You don't have to do that," Adam said, his heart beginning to pound a little faster even as his own words were falling out of his mouth. "I told you, you have resources, and I'm one of them."

His heart was shocked at the decision his brain had made so hastily. Or, maybe his heart had made the decision without any brain input. Either way, Adam was not all together. He couldn't be, or his ears wouldn't have just heard his mouth say what it said.

There was an extended silence. Before Adam could use the empty time to question his own wisdom, before he could remind himself that Molly was precisely the kind of woman he could never make this sort of monumental decision with, he said, "I do believe this is literally a pregnant pause."

"I'm just trying to take the time I need to make sure I did not misunderstand you," Molly answered slowly.

"I apologize for not being totally clear," Adam said. "What I meant to say was, let's get married."

He thought at first that the thud in his ear was his conscience trying to beat some sense into his skull. A half moment later, he realized it was the loud echo of Molly's abrupt disconnection.

Molly stared wide-eyed at the phone lying on the ground next to the wall, where she'd flung it as if it had spontaneously combusted next to her ear.

A second later, she scrambled over to snatch it off the floor and dialed Adam's number. "Oops," she said when he answered on the first half ring. "I, uh, I dropped the phone." She shrugged one shoulder as if he could see it in his apartment twenty miles away.

"Of course."

"So I missed the rest of your joke."

"What joke?"

"You—you said, 'Let's get marr-marr—'" Molly cleared her throat. "You said—"

"Let's get married."

Hearing those words in Adam's voice, did things as weird and foreign to her insides as the baby did. "Right, and then I hung up on the punch line."

"There was no punch line."

"Adam, can you cease and desist with the games right now? I had a hell of a day, and—"

"No games. I'm dead serious. We always said we'd marry each other anyway if we didn't have better offers."

Molly didn't remind him that that agreement was supposed to go into effect when they turned thirty, and then in a semidrunken panic at his surprise party, they had mutually declared that pact null and void, at least until they hit forty.

What did it say about her that it was the closest she'd ever gotten to a marriage proposal? Well, until two minutes ago.

"Just for one year," Adam went on. "The term of your job. What's the big deal? Unless you have a boyfriend these days that I also have no idea about."

"No."

"Well, I don't have a girlfriend at present. So I repeat, what's the big deal? We'll go to a justice of the peace, get married, you'll get your great job, everyone's happy."

"What'll you get out of it?"

He paused. "Helping you. We're best friends. That's *my* job."

"This would have to be a serious secret," Molly warned. "I mean, serious. I wouldn't even tell my friends and neighbors the truth. I'm a terrible liar. If I tell one story to everyone, it'll be easier."

"Agreed."

"Marry Adam Shibbs?" Molly mumbled. "Oh, that was meant to be internal dialogue," she said, louder. "Sorry."

"Hey," he said, wounded. "I happen to know dozens of women who would love to marry me."

"I'm sorry." She paused. "I mean, we'd have to live together to keep this up. You'd have to live here."

"You can come here, if you prefer."

"No, there's more room here and this is my—well, this is my house. I don't want to be somewhere else. Especially while I'm pregnant."

"Understood."

"You'd be moving into my house," she reiterated, and then she sank to the floor. She leaned her back against the wall and stretched her legs out in front of her. "We're overlooking the small fact that we annoy the crap out of each other."

"True. But I think this is important enough for us to compromise."

"We can't compromise our personalities, can we? For a whole year? We're so different." *Which is why we've never even attempted to date,* she added silently. *Which is why we're best friends.*

Adam didn't answer, and Molly realized he wouldn't. He knew she could argue him into the ground on any point. So he'd rested his case, and it was now up to her.

Marry Adam?

It would be in name only. She knew he'd stick to the rules they set. But wasn't marriage supposed to be something more, something about love?

She *did* love Adam. But not in the to-have-and-to-hold way. More like in the to-have-fun-and-to-hold-good-parties-with way. Right. She put a hand over her chest, felt the pounding of her heart. And that, that was merely because she was surprised.

It didn't seem right to compromise on marriage. If she was ever going to bother taking this kind of step, it should be for the right, idealistic reasons.

"I can't," she finally said. "Adam, I can't. Because you're my friend, my real friend. Which you're proving by offering to make this kind of sacrifice. And I will be grateful to you forever, but I just can't."

Adam still didn't respond, and Molly thought for an impossible moment that she might have really hurt him, that he felt rejected. A little pain stabbed at her heart. Then he said, "All right. I thought it was a good idea, but it's just as well. I've heard that you snore."

It was a typical Adam comment, but the last word

fell a tiny bit flat. "I'd better go," Molly said. "I'm hungry again, which is not to be believed. And, Adam…thank you."

"Don't say thank you. Saying no to a marriage proposal is one thing. Saying 'no, thanks' to a marriage proposal is another."

Molly said a hasty goodbye and hung up. She put her head in her hands, and didn't realize she was crying again until she felt the tears leak out from between her fingers and drip down her wrist. Stupid hormones. If it hadn't been for all her uncharacteristic boo-hooing, Adam wouldn't have lost his mind and proposed, she wouldn't have said no, and things wouldn't be all strange between them now.

But she couldn't do what he was suggesting. Even if it wasn't *really* real. Adam was not the man she was supposed to marry. She was supposed to marry a man just like her—ambitious and career-oriented, someone who understood her goals not because she had to explain them, but because he had similar ones. That's what her parents had in each other. That's why Molly had been one of the only children in her small, elite private grade school with still-married parents. She'd emulated them in so many ways, so why not this important one?

"It's worth waiting for," she whispered to her baby, but why did it feel as if she were trying to convince herself? Her eyes overflowed again.

Plunk.

It was the sound of a large drop hitting the floor. A drop too heavy to be a tear.

Plunk.

This time, Molly was looking straight ahead and caught sight of the drop hitting her hardwood floor about six inches in front of her. She got onto her hands and knees, crawled to the spot, looked at the little puddle and sat back on her heels and tilted her head up to peer at the ceiling.

Plunk.

This drop didn't hit the floor. It hit Molly's large stomach. She stared at the spot on her sweater.

The ceiling was leaking. *Leaking.*

She jumped up awkwardly, scrambled into her office and turned over her wastebasket. Crumpled sticky notes and receipts skittered across the floor as she carried the bucket to the hallway, positioning it under the leak, which had quickened into a more regular *plunk-plunk-plunk.*

A freaking ceiling leak. This was going to cost—well, she couldn't even guess. All she knew was, roof leaks were not cheap. She was *really* going to call that inspector she'd used and give him a piece of her mind.

She glanced down again at the wet spot on her shirt, and rubbed it with her hand. Her eyes welled up again.

No. This was going to be under control. She could do this. She was going to be an excellent mother. She was going to be as good at it as she was at everything else. And she was *not* going to let it rain on her little baby's head.

She would do whatever it took to keep her future, and the future of her child, secure. And dry.

She snatched the phone off the floor where she'd left it, and hit redial. When Adam answered, she said, "Here's the thing. If you think you're going to be entitled to any special, ah, privileges of marriage, you will be mistaken."

A beat. "Too bad," he said. "I was kind of looking forward to complaining about my mother-in-law."

"That's not the privilege I'm referring to and you damn well know it."

"Didn't this conversation end already with you saying no?"

"I take it back."

"Pardon?"

Molly took a deep breath, squeezed her eyes shut, and told her best friend, "It's a deal. For one year, you've got yourself a wife."

Chapter Three

Most Saturday mornings, Adam woke up with ideas in his head about how he was going to spend a fun weekend. Basketball with the guys, a romp in the park with Elmer, trying out a new restaurant, taking in an action flick, watching a ball game on TV with a large sausage pizza. Some weekends, he could cram all those things in, if he wanted to. Or he could spend two days sitting in an armchair reading books about topics he'd discovered he found interesting so that by Monday morning, he was a pseudo-expert.

This was definitely the first Saturday morning when he awoke, blinked at the sunlight streaming in on either side of the window shade, and thought, I need to pack a suitcase so I can go get married.

He squinted at the glowing red numbers on his clock. After ten already. Well, he'd been up kind of late. He'd figured he should remain near the phone in case Molly called him back and changed her mind again.

She hadn't. And he'd stayed on his sofa through two and a half lame infomercials just to be sure.

He rolled out of bed and onto his knees on the floor. He stretched his hands over his head and let out a loud groan, then reached under his bed and slid out his suitcase. He blew a dust bunny off the top of it and Elmer, who'd been quietly sitting in the corner, chased it back under the bed.

Adam heaved the bag onto the still-warm sheets and opened it. He really didn't know how much to pack. A little piece of him was feeling as if this were a dream. It was a pretty big suitcase, though. He decided to pack it until it was full.

He emptied two large dresser drawers next to the bag, then picked a pair of jeans out of the pile and slid them on his body, leaving the top button open. Then he began to fold without giving much thought to each garment. His brain was filled with Molly, and what she was thinking this morning, but in all the time he'd known that woman, he could never guess what she was thinking.

He wondered if husbands were supposed to know

what their wives were thinking. Probably not, but their guesses were likely to be at least in the ballpark.

Right now, he felt like the starting pitcher in a game he wasn't even originally supposed to play.

He rolled up several T-shirts and tossed them in the bag, picking up his pace, trying to keep his mind busy so it wouldn't amuse itself with any more bad baseball analogies.

Should he pack towels? Molly would have lots of towels, but could he presume he'd be using them? Would marriage entitle him to towel usage? What about sheets?

Where was he going to sleep, anyway? And why didn't he think about all this *before* he proposed?

"This is too much," Adam muttered in Elmer's direction. Elmer responded by pricking up his ears, then bounding out of the room.

Adam was shaking out his brown corduroy pants and hoping for a supernatural sign that he was doing the right thing when he heard his name ring out.

"Adam! Where are you?"

For a moment, he allowed himself the luxury of thinking that the divine was summoning him for a heart-to-heart. But unless the divine was taking the form of his mother's voice, that wasn't to be.

"Uncle Adam!" The voices of Trevor and Billy, his nephews, echoed through the small apartment, followed by his sister's bellowing. "Where the heck are you? Still sleeping?"

Last night's monumental events had completely erased his memory of his family's scheduled visit this morning. He couldn't let them see he was packing. He wasn't in the mood for questions right now, and he couldn't logically sort things out for them before he sorted them out for himself.

He rushed out of his bedroom and slammed the door hard behind him, colliding head-on with Janine.

"Watch it, buddy," his sister said. "You forgot we were coming, didn't you?"

"Heck, no. You wound me."

"Then you were so excited to see us, you forgot to put on a shirt?"

"That's right."

She hugged him and patted his bare shoulders. "Nice to see you."

"You, too." His sister's brown hair was smushed into a girly ponytail thing, which looked cute but was not the kind of thing she would have done with her hair before having kids. He remembered her hours with the hair dryer and curling iron, leaving Adam to hop up and down outside the bathroom, waiting. His sister was still pretty, but in a softer, less deliberate way.

Trevor and Billy flew into Adam, their collisions purposeful. "Oof."

"Uncle Adam," Trevor said with all the urgency of an eight-year-old. "I got a goal in soccer. It went right over the goalie's head."

Not to be outdone, ten-year-old Billy cut in. "I got first seat trumpet in band this year. I beat all the sixth-graders. I can't wait for school to start."

"That's a new one," Janine mumbled, rumpling both her sons' hair.

"You guys rock," Adam said. "I have the coolest nephews ever."

They both grinned, and although blond Trevor and dark-haired Billy didn't look much alike at first glance, their smiles were nearly identical.

"I love it when all my kids are in one place," he heard, and the kids stepped aside to let Adam's mother hug him. "How are you?"

"Same, no change," Adam said, inhaling his mother's classic French perfume, the kind he got her for Mother's Day every year, as she rested her head of brunette curls on his chest. He glanced guiltily at the closed bedroom door. "Let's go see what I have to eat."

"Probably nothing, as usual," Pam said. "So we brought plenty." She headed to the kitchen, two hungry kids scampering behind. Adam went to follow them, but turned to check the door one last time.

It was open, and Janine was stepping out into the hall.

"What are you doing?" Adam asked.

"Tossing my sweater on your bed, where I always put it."

"Why are you wearing a sweater? It's like eighty-five degrees outside."

"Why are you packing? Are you going somewhere?"

Adam pushed his sister back into his room and kicked the door shut.

"Oh," Janine squealed, balling her fists in excitement. "It's a secret. What is it?"

"None of your business," Adam said, pulling on a black T-shirt and trying to sound fierce enough for his sister to back off. He should have known it would only intrigue her further.

"Tell me what's going on," she insisted, her threatening tone matching his. She was only a year older than him, but somehow she always managed to make it seem as if it were much more.

"Or what?"

She narrowed her eyes. "Or I'm telling Mom."

"What are you, five? Besides, you don't even know what you're telling her," Adam countered, getting a bit nervous.

"I don't have to. I'll just tell her something's up and she'll drag it out of you."

Adam knew she was right. "Janine, I'm serious."

"So am I. You can't just be taking off somewhere, all cloak-and-dagger, with like a month's worth of clothes, and leave us here to worry about you."

"I'm not going far."

"Where's not far?"

The two siblings glared at each other in a silent

standoff, until Janine broke it by throwing open the door and yelling, "Mom!"

"You're not even my real sister," Adam said in juvenile desperation. "Mom and Dad just felt sorry for you when your spaceship left without you, and they took you in."

Janine put her hands on her hips. "For your information, I didn't even believe that when I was a kid."

"Yes, you did."

"No, I didn't," she said, "because I happen to know for a fact that a pack of mangy wolves left you on our doorstep when you were a baby."

"Really?" asked Trevor, who had come into the room without the adults noticing. "You're a wolf, Uncle Adam?"

"I'm not just any wolf," Adam told his towheaded nephew. "I'm the Big Bad Wolf." He howled menacingly and lunged, causing Trevor to shriek. Elmer bounded in and added his puppy howls to the fray. Laughing, Janine joined in. Billy ran in to see what the racket was about and began howling too without knowing why.

An earsplitting whistle pierced the air, and the noise abruptly ceased.

"It's clear I raised a bunch of wild animals," Pam said to the silence. A few giggles came from the two boys.

"Billy and Trevor," Pam said, "go to the living room and take Elmer with you." She turned to the two adults, and Adam detected a twinkle in her eye. "Watch TV for a few minutes. I need to talk to my children."

The boys, snickering the way kids did when they saw their elders being treated like fellow kids, edged out of the room, Billy gently tugging a still-scrabbling Elmer by the collar.

Adam marveled, and certainly not for the first time, at how his mother, the epitome of homespun living, could put an effective smackdown on a roomful of misbehavior.

"Mom," Janine said. "Adam has something to tell you."

"Space-alien girl," Adam muttered.

"What is it?" Pam demanded of her son. When he didn't answer, she scanned the room for a hint, and saw the open suitcase, half filled with T-shirts and boxer shorts. She addressed her daughter. "What is going on?"

Janine shrugged, eyeballing her brother.

Adam threw up his hands in defeat, and walked over to the suitcase. He had plenty to do, and he really couldn't afford to waste any more time.

"I'm moving out for a little while," he said. "And I fully intended to tell you. Janine, I was going to ask you if you want to stay here with the boys and keep an eye on the place. For free. I'll keep up the rent."

Janine appeared suddenly ecstatic. Adam knew she'd hated to impose on their mother by having to stay with her since her recent divorce. Although Adam suspected Pam didn't mind in the least.

"For how long?" Janine asked.

"Oh," Adam said, trying to sound nonchalant, "about a year."

"A year?" Janine yelled.

"Did you get some kind of transfer?" his mother asked, and Adam noticed she was trying to stay calm. He hastened his explanation.

"No, I'm going to stay with Molly for a while."

Both women stared at him. "Is Molly okay?" Pam asked. "She's not sick, is she?"

"No, not exactly. She's kind of—well, pregnant."

Silence.

Adam began folding clothes faster. "So I'm going to marry her for a little while. It's not a big deal."

The silence continued, and when he ventured a glance up, both women had their mouths wide open.

"She's pregnant?" Janine finally asked. "She—you and she—"

"No," Adam interrupted. "Not me. I'm not the father."

"But you're marrying her?" Pam asked. "So you're in love with her?"

"No," Adam said quickly. "Absolutely not in love. Just helping out. Best-friend duty."

"Why?" Janine asked. "Molly seems too sensible for weirdness like this. And you, Mr. Serial Dater, making any commitment for longer than twelve hours stuns me."

"Thanks a lot."

"I'm just saying."

"Look," Adam said, raking his hands through his hair and looking at his family, "I can't tell you any more than that. I promised her. She's in a situation, she needs help, and no one is supposed to know this marriage isn't a real one."

"But it will be a real one," Pam pointed out.

"I mean, a marriage based on—on…"

"On love?" Janine asked.

Adam said nothing.

"Because," his sister went on, "after all, you are not in love with her."

"I'm not in love with her," Adam repeated through gritted teeth. "How many times will I have to say that?"

"Probably about once a day," Pam said, "if you're going to be married and living under the same roof."

Adam wished his mother weren't so smart, because then he could just ignore her, instead of experiencing an uneasy internal foreshadowing.

"So, when can we move in here?" Janine asked.

"I'm going over to Molly's tonight. But I'll have to keep coming back for my stuff every now and then."

"Sure."

"When are you and Molly actually getting married?" Pam inquired, sitting on the edge of the bed and picking up a pair of already folded khakis. She unfolded them, shook them out and folded them in a much neater, expert way.

"I'm not absolutely sure. Some time next week?"

"Well, as long as the mother of the groom gets a little advance notice."

"Mom," he said. "This isn't that kind of wedding."

"Every wedding is that kind of wedding," Pam informed her son. "I intend to be there."

"Me, too," Janine said. "Did you get rings?"

"I haven't even gotten breakfast," Adam said. "This was all decided less than fifteen hours ago."

"You need rings," Janine said.

"And flowers," Pam said.

"Molly's going to kill me that you guys even know about this," Adam said.

His mother looked surprised. "Surely Molly didn't think you weren't going to tell your family you got married?"

"Well, she didn't want anyone to know it's not really for real."

"But you haven't told us practically anything," Janine said reasonably. "Besides, we won't breathe a word. Because what if you guys actually do fall in love?"

Adam dropped his travel alarm clock on the floor and it buzzed shrilly. He picked it up and fumbled with it. "We won't," he said over the din. How did something this small make so much noise? Where was the damn button? He found it and the clock quieted in his hands. He almost said, *We won't, because not only did I decide long ago, when Dad died, that I wouldn't live like him, but I also decided I wouldn't love anyone who lived like him. And Molly is so, so like him.* Instead, he just cut the reply down to, "We won't."

His mother and his sister met each other's eyes.

"Do not do that," he said.

"Do what?" they both asked him.

"Give each other that female *look*. You know what I'm talking about."

"How is Molly feeling?" Pam asked, deftly taking control of the conversation. "How far along is she?"

"I guess fine. Six months."

Pam looked taken aback. "Six months already? And you didn't know about this at all?"

"I haven't talked to her in about that long."

"Well, if she needs a hand with anything at all, tell her she can always call your sister or me for professional mother advice."

"She won't have to. She's Molly. She's got everything under control."

Pam's eyebrows disappeared underneath her wispy bangs. "You think a woman going through her first pregnancy, and perhaps an unexpected one at that, a woman who also runs her own business and not too long ago bought her own home, has got everything 'under control'?"

Adam paused midfold and ruminated a moment.

Molly popped into his head—pinstriped, efficiently quick-moving Molly, holding a stack of folders in one hand and a phone in the other. "Sure."

Then his mental picture suddenly warped and changed. Molly's midsection expanded, popping two blazer buttons. Overwhelming tears rolled down her cheeks, the shocking tears he'd heard on the phone. The tears that drove him to propose marriage to a woman who was his polar opposite in every imaginable way.

"Sure," he repeated, but this time the word sounded a little bit false.

This plan had made a whole lot more sense before his family started asking questions.

Hadn't it?

He bent and dragged a pair of sneakers off his closet floor, and emerged just in time to see Janine and Pam exchange another one of those looks, but this time Adam deliberately ignored it. Just because they had a history of always being right, didn't mean they would be right when it came to Molly. Or him.

Adam parked in front of Molly's house, but Molly, absorbed in the garden patch underneath a front window with her back to him, didn't appear to hear his car. He sat and watched her.

The muscles in her back worked underneath her thin white T-shirt as she bent over doing who knew what in the dirt. Every few seconds, she flipped her dark masses of curls over her shoulder, only to have them slip down her front again. And every few minutes, she toppled over.

She was sitting on a little stool low to the ground, and she seemed to be having a difficult time keeping her balance. She kept catching herself before actually hitting the grass, but he could interpret the mounting frustration in her body, just a little bit more with each time she righted herself. He didn't have to see the expression of grim determination on her face to know it was there. It was her most popular look.

When he saw her pick up a little shovel and fling it with annoyance to the ground, sending bits of soil flying, he decided it was time to save her from herself.

He got out of his car and slammed the door. Her head snapped around. Now, *that* look, Adam thought, was not a familiar one on Molly. Nervous, unsure, lacking confidence and maybe even a little…scared.

He raised his hand in greeting and she got to her feet, kicking the stool away from her. She turned, and—

Whoa.

She approached him, and a wry smile curved up one corner of her top lip. She tugged down the hem of her shirt as she walked. "Notice anything different about me?" she asked when she stopped in front of him.

"Just the most obvious thing," Adam answered. "Nice rack."

Molly's eyes widened, but then she crossed her arms over her breasts and, Adam noticed, tried and failed to not look pleased. She'd complained as long as he'd known her about what she called her hereditary flat chest, and although he'd never found her physically lacking in any way whatsoever, he had a feeling that she'd consider pregnancy breasts a bonus.

The truth was, there was quite a lot different about Molly today, and it wasn't just her breasts or the swell of her midsection. Her hair seemed thicker somehow, curls a man could lose his hands in if he ventured to touch them. And her skin, always smooth and clear, seemed somehow purified, bright, like a light had been switched on inside her and was radiating out from every pore on her face, her neck, her arms. A trickle of perspiration ran down between her collarbone and disappeared into the new crevice between her suddenly lush breasts, and Adam felt his own upper lip grow damp in response.

He blinked.

For years, he'd had physical reactions to Molly. A man would have to be blind and deaf and one hundred percent oblivious not to be affected by her in any way. But the reaction was different now, stronger, needier, now that he was faced with the softer, more feminine, more vulnerable Molly. The woman that he was about to marry and live with for a year.

He swallowed and waited for her to speak, but she didn't appear to know what to say next, either, so they stood regarding each other in silence.

He saw her eyes travel down to his shoulders,

down his torso, all the way down to his beat-up sneakers and back up again. Her neutral expression didn't change, and Adam supposed that was a plus. She could have curled her lip in disgust, thinking, *This lazy, unmotivated guy who makes me mental is going to save my career?*

It's you who doesn't understand me, Adam thought back at her. *You don't know why I am the way I am because I never told you. I never told you everything about my father because I don't talk about that, ever, with anyone.*

But, he continued in his mind, *I will rescue you. I will be the hero because I have a feeling this is the only time in your life that you ever needed one.*

"Want to see the house?" Molly asked, and Adam was startled at the subject change before he realized it wasn't one, that they hadn't been really communicating and that his assurances to her were still only in his head.

"Sure," he said, and allowed her to lead him inside. "What were you planting?"

"Mums."

"That's appropriate. Mums for a new mum. If, you know, you were British."

Molly chuckled at the weak joke and ushered him through her front door.

The last time he'd been to Molly's Danbury Way home, she'd just moved in and there were neatly taped, unpacked boxes stacked in almost every corner. Now the boxes were gone and every room was vibrant with color and style—ruby and saffron pillows piled on the sofa, tiny bud vases on end tables sprouting pussy willows, shaggy, ropey throw rugs on the shining wood floors. A stranger would instantly know that Molly paid obsessive attention to the smallest details, and that this house was a manifestation of a longtime dream of how a home should be. Molly's sweeping hand gesture as they entered the warm living room, the sunny kitchen and the flowery bathroom, conveyed her pride in her hard work.

In all the rooms—except one.

At the top of the stairs, next to her bedroom, one door remained shut.

"What's in here?" Adam inquired, opening the door.

"Oh," Molly said, "that's the nursery."

Not that you could tell. The walls were a flawless white, the window covered only with open blinds. Early-evening light angled in between the slats, illuminating the bereft emptiness of the rest of the room.

"Doesn't look much like a nursery yet," Adam said, and his voice echoed back at him, bouncing off the clean, bare walls.

"It's my next project," Molly said quickly. "I just haven't gotten quite around to it yet."

"Clearly." Adam was baffled. If he listened hard, he was certain he'd hear the desolate sound of chirping crickets.

"I'll get it done," Molly said, a slight defensiveness edging into her voice.

When? he wondered, but what he said was, "Of course you will."

Hmm.

They went back downstairs, Adam bounding down first, and then waiting for Molly to continue her slower progress. It was the first time he could ever remember that he moved faster than she did.

"Want to go out and get some dinner?" he suggested. "You can show me around town."

"You don't need me to show you Rosewood," Molly said. "You were the one that suggested this town to me in the first place when I decided to buy a house."

"No, no, I meant, you can show me around to the town. Maybe we'll see some people you know."

Her face paled a little from her healthy glow.

"I'll put on a different shirt," he offered.

"No, that one's nice," she said. She reached out and touched the dark green cotton, absentmindedly rubbing. He fought the surprising urge to catch her hand and still her restless fingers.

She shrugged. "I thought you would come here and tell me you changed your mind."

"Did you want me to?"

"No. Well, yes. Or—no."

She sank down onto her sofa, and Adam sat across from her in a comfortable leather armchair.

"My suitcase is in the car," he said. "Just tell me

if you want me to go get it. Or I can leave it, and take it home with me after dinner."

Molly gazed out the window for a few moments. "You haven't thought this through."

"On the contrary. I've thought this through more than I've ever thought anything through in my life. I just did it quickly. You don't have the luxury of time." He nodded at her middle. "He doesn't, either. Or she. He or she?"

"I don't know."

"You don't know? How are you going to plan and organize if you don't know?"

She cocked her head. "I'm not that bad."

"Yeah, you are."

"Well, hey, the baby was a surprise. So I figured, might as well go surprise all the way."

He grinned. "That would have been my choice, too."

"I know. Or, I mean, I could have guessed." She sighed and reached up to massage her own shoulders.

Adam noticed she was even more hunched over than usual. Years of stressful bending over desks and computers had permanently curved her long ago, so that even when she was standing her tallest and proudest five foot seven, she resembled a long graceful cattail bending into a persistent summer breeze.

"Maybe I'm the one who hasn't thought this through," she said.

"Yes, you have," Adam said. "You just haven't found a million reasons to object. Because there are hardly any. I'm not someone you never met, and this isn't an arranged marriage expected to last a lifetime. This is on our own terms."

She nodded. Adam didn't stop to consider the irony of his having to be the one to convince Molly this whole plan wasn't insane when he was the one who'd been consumed every minute since he'd arrived by stunningly lustful thoughts. And the challenge of being under the same roof for a year…

He forged on. "We're just breaking a few social rules," he said. "Who cares?"

"Yeah," Molly said, still nodding. "Who cares? We're adults. We can do things the way we need to, tweak the world to fit our needs."

"Exactly. Now you've got it."

"And we don't have to justify it to anyone."

"Right."

"No one knows but us."

"Uh," Adam said. "Well. Us, and my mom and my sister." He deliberately mumbled his last few words, but Molly exploded.

"You told your mother and Janine?"

"They do not know the whole story. That is to say, they do not know your story. They know that we're getting married, and it's probably temporary, and they know you're pregnant and I had nothing to do with it, but that's it."

"Adam, I swear—"

"I trust them," he said.

"I trusted *you,*" she retorted.

"They're going to be your family, too," Adam said. "At least for a little while. And they're happy for you, and they want to help you, and us. Please."

Molly pressed her lips together. Adam thought about Molly's parents, and the one time he'd met them. They'd come to the graduation of their only child, and when Adam watched Molly proudly show them her degree, they nodded with satisfaction, as if she were a thoroughbred that had been favored to win the Kentucky Derby and was now draped in roses. There were no hugs, no kisses. The support was present, but it was in the form of expectations and funding for the accomplishment, not love and joy for the milestone. Their faces were determined, eyes on the prizes.

All three Jacksons looked, Adam had thought then, the way his own father used to look, before and after work. Dad had only been dead about four years then, and Pam had cried with happiness that day at the sight of her son in black cap and gown, overcome with enough emotion for two parents. Still, Adam remembered now, a crucial piece had been missing for him that day.

Adam's mother and sister adored Molly in a way that he realized Molly had to get used to over the years, and Adam trusted now that it had become something important to her.

The anger dissolved from her face, and her lips

eventually relaxed. "All right. But no one else. Or I'll never be able to pull this off."

"I promise. And you're not pulling off anything. The two of us are."

A fluttering moved Molly's T-shirt, and Adam thought he was imagining things until he stared another minute and it happened again. "Is that for real? Did I just see that?"

"Yeah."

He slid off the chair and scooted over on the floor to sit at her feet. "Can I?"

She hesitated only a fraction of an instant. "Yes."

He laid his palm flat over the thin material of her shirt and waited against her warmth. Then he felt it, a bumping against his hand, a purposeful greeting.

"Hey there, baby," Adam whispered. "Let me amend what I said." He looked at Molly's suddenly flushed face. "The *three* of us will pull this off."

"Bring in your suitcase," Molly whispered back.

Chapter Four

"Adam, stop."

Adam stepped away from the door to Entrée and waited, watching Molly.

She peered into the trendy, quaint bistro and fought a wave of panic. Normally, she loved coming here when it was busy. But tonight, as almost every Saturday night, the crowd would surely contain at least one person she knew. Probably more than one.

Maybe a few months from now, the lying would feel like second nature—being out in public with Adam, disguised as a loving married couple—but on this, their possible debut evening, Molly felt like a rank novice at the art of deception.

Meanwhile, Adam, who as far as she knew had never told even the smallest lie, seemed perfectly at ease, like a trained spy on a reconnaissance mission. One of his hands was loose in his pocket, the other dangling at his side. Molly's hands wrung and twisted at each other.

"It's going to be fine," Adam said.

"Aren't you nervous?"

"Only that the food won't be as good as you said it is."

Molly examined his face, and detected a teeny, tiny twitch at the outer corner of his right eye. Aha, she thought. That's lie number one.

Well, okay. She could do this. She'd just keep this dinner low key.

They entered the restaurant, and the soft sound of live jazz filtered in from the lounge area. Despite the relaxing ambiance, Molly tensed a bit as Marti Vincente, the hostess, flashed her trademark welcoming smile.

"Molly!" she cried, as if it hadn't been only about two weeks since Molly had been to Entrée. Marti's red hair glowed golden, reflecting the romantic candles lit around the room. "You look positively gorgeous," she said. "Best pregnant woman I've ever seen. You haven't even lost that adorable little figure yet, which means you won't, you lucky thing. You look more like you just ate a big meal."

It was such a lovely and kind fib, Molly hated to

argue with it. "Not yet, but I am looking forward to a big meal."

"Great specials tonight. The usual table?" Then Marti gave a start, noticing Adam. "Oh!"

"This is Adam Shibbs," Molly said, trying not to trip over her words. "He's my—um—"

"Date," Adam said smoothly.

"Marti Vincente. We live three doors down from Molly. My husband Ed and I own this place."

"Judging by the number of customers, you're doing a great job."

Marti preened. "We think so," she said, and laughed good-naturedly. She turned back to Molly. "Well, then, let's seat you two by the window. A table just opened up and a cute couple like you is sure to bring in more business if passersby can see you."

"We won't even complain about the ulterior motive if the specials are as great as you say," Adam said.

Marti laughed again and grabbed two menus. "They are. Especially the veal. Here we go." She gestured toward the most obvious table in the entire restaurant, Molly noticed with dismay. People in their living rooms across the street would be able to see the flavor of salad dressing she chose. Marti was enthusiastic and sweet, Molly thought, but so much for low-key.

"Nice meeting you, Adam. Enjoy, Molly."

"Nice meeting you, too, Marti," Adam said. Molly's smile hurt a little bit.

She opened up the oversize menu and ducked behind it, peeking out just enough to check out their fellow diners. She noticed Judith and Sam Martin, her neighbors on the opposite end of Danbury Way, at a corner table. Judith's young, striking face was arranged into a scowl in her husband's direction, as usual. Sam broke a breadstick with more force than Molly imagined necessary, spattering crumbs onto the clean tablecloth. Well, those two never noticed much outside their own bickering, so that wasn't too bad. Thankfully, she didn't seem to recognize anyone else here tonight. Maybe if she and Adam ate really fast, before anyone else came in…

"You must come here often if you have a usual table," Adam remarked.

Molly didn't move her menu. She stared at the elaborate script, too close to her face to actually read. "Every couple of weeks," she said. "But I like to come alone, and there's this nice small private table in the back, so I sit there a lot to work while I eat."

"That's the most depressing thing I ever heard."

"There's nothing wrong with eating alone," Molly said into the menu.

His hand appeared over the spine of the menu and pulled it down to the table. Adam smiled. "Hi there. I didn't mean eating alone. That's great. What I mean is working while you're eating."

"I multitask."

"That's the problem. You should concentrate on eating. Eating is its own reward."

"Spoken like someone who doesn't have another person taking up residence inside him who is hungry every second of the day."

"Clearly, your baby already understands the value of a slow, savory meal. That's one smart kid."

"Or one with your tendency to be a total person of leisure."

"You say that like it's a bad thing."

"It's not a productive thing."

"I don't need to be productive," Adam said, showing no signs of being offended. "The world around me produces plenty. I enjoy. I partake."

"Maybe what you need is a new job. If you liked your job more—"

She cut herself off as the waitress came by and cheerfully took their drink orders. When they were alone, she started again. "Maybe if you—"

"I heard you. I like my job just fine. The food company's great. Nice people. It's just not my life."

"Maybe middle management isn't challenging enough for you."

"Maybe it's just something I do to pay my bills and I like having plenty of time for other pursuits. Good wine, good food, music, sports, reading, my friends, my family. I'm not like you."

"I know. We've had this discussion, I suppose."

"You're allowed to have it one more time with me,

now, as my fiancée," he conceded. "Then, when you're my wife, I'll even let you engage me in this conversation one more time as a concerned spouse. But I will not change my ways. You, on the other hand, might have to."

"Excuse me?"

The waitress returned and set their drinks down. "I'll give you two a few more minutes," she said, and wisely scurried away upon glancing at Molly's face.

"You have a baby coming," Adam said, "who isn't going to be as interested in M.J. Consulting as you are. You might have to, well, chill out a little."

"How very Stone Age. I'm fully capable of being a mother and having a career."

"I'd never assume you're not capable of that. But you're also fully capable of total burnout. I'm not suggesting you give anything up. Just scale back a little for a while." He held up his hand as she heaved a readying breath. "Just a little, I said, because I'm going to be there to help you out. One benefit of working for a major conglomerate is they're very progressive about things like paternity leave. Hello," he said to the waitress, who was hovering by. "I'd like the veal special upon Mrs. Vincente's suggestion."

"And for you, ma'am?"

Paternity leave? He was going to take time out from work to take care of her baby?

"I would never ask you to do that," she said to Adam.

"You didn't have to ask me. I ordered the veal because it sounds delicious."

"No, I mean you don't have to feel like you have to do that for me."

"Okay, then we'll split the check."

"Ma'am?" the waitress prompted again.

Molly pointed to a random pasta dish on the menu, and the waitress appeared relieved to take their order away.

"I'm talking about your leave," Molly said.

"I know you are, but I already made the decision."

"What if you need the leave for your own reasons?"

"Your baby is my reason."

His selflessness was astounding. So much so, in fact, that Molly was having a hard time accepting it. "Do you know how to take care of a baby?"

"Do you?"

"Um," Molly said, biting her lip. "Sure I do."

"Me, too," Adam said. "As you know, I have two nephews that I've helped out a lot with for years. Plus I have Elmer."

"Elmer would be who, exactly?"

"My dog. You're going to love him."

"You're bringing a dog to live in my house?"

"He's hardly even a dog. He's a little puppy furball. I left him at my place tonight because the boys wanted to spend the night with him."

"You didn't tell me you got a puppy."

"Do you really want to go down this road of

what we neglected to tell each other in the last couple of months?"

Molly mopped up some olive oil with a roll and stuffed half of it into her mouth.

"Besides," he said with a grin, "Elmer can be like a practice kid. You can feed him and hug him and scold him when he misbehaves. Although he won't pay any attention. He ignores all my attempts at discipline."

"Then I guess that would make him more of a practice teenager."

"Touché," Adam said, chuckling.

Adam's smile was different now than when she'd met him in college, she noticed through the flickering candlelight. It was just as frequent as it had always been, but it was set deeper into his face somehow. Years of mischief and boyish charm had etched permanent small lines around his eyes and mouth, so that even when he was serious, evidence of smiling remained. His eyes were a bright green, such a nearly impossible color that Molly had once insisted Adam poke his finger against his eyeball to prove he didn't actually wear contacts. She hadn't been sure which was more impressive—that the green was true or that he had actually taken her up on her dare.

"Why so quiet?" Adam asked.

"Just preparing to enjoy a slow, savory dinner."

"Touché again. You're pretty funny when you want to be. I taught you well."

"It's inborn, Shibbs, not learned." She took a long drink of water, draining half her glass in one gulp. "Can we talk about something else for a while? I mean, something other than our dubious future."

"Or our perceived character flaws?"

"Yeah. Just talk about whatever you want. Engage me in witty repartee."

"Well, I saw this special on hammerhead sharks on TV the other night. Do you know what they look like?"

"I don't think so."

One thing about Adam, he never lacked a topic for conversation. It was as if he knew a bit of something about everything. And perhaps relieved of deep relationship discussion, they covered close to everything, right through their dinners and down to their crème brûlée.

By then, things were almost back to normal between them. Easy, fun, friendly. No pressure. The tension eased out of Molly with each bite she took, with each laugh, with each familiar grin that passed between her and Adam.

When Molly lifted the last forkful to her mouth, Adam grabbed her wrist. "Stop. Save that for last. I have something for you first."

He reached into his pocket and pulled out a tiny box. "Please don't get mad."

Molly couldn't take her eyes off the box, so she didn't see Adam get up and come to her side until he was on one knee, his face level with hers.

"Oh, my God," she said.

"Please forgive me, but—" He opened the box, and inside was nestled a pure round sparkle.

"Oh, my God!" shrieked Marti from the middle of the restaurant, causing every single person in the nearly filled-to-capacity place to turn to the picture window and take in the romantic scene framed there.

"Oh, my God," Molly whispered.

"Molly Jackson," Adam asked, "will you marry me?"

Adam Shibbs was on one knee. Adam Shibbs was holding her hand. Adam Shibbs was asking her to be his wife in front of half of Rosewood.

Adam Shibbs's voice was shaking.

She just nodded, and the room burst into applause and cheers and joyful laughter. Adam slid the ring onto her finger, then stood and swept her out of her chair and into his arms.

Her lips pressed into his ear. "That had better be cubic z," she hissed through her smile.

"I'm no cheap bastard."

"You bought me a diamond ring? Why?" She squeezed his shoulders harder, and the crowd clapped more. "When? Why?"

"Today," he said. "And because."

She pulled back and stared at him, then buried her head into his neck again and said into his other ear, "You shouldn't have done this. Not in public, and not yet. What if I don't get the job?"

"That's not even possible." He broke their embrace this time, and his green eyes held hers. "Molly, you are the best at everything you do. I have faith in you. This is my faith in you."

Molly, overcome by her ring, their audience and in learning how it felt to have a man believe in her even more than she believed in herself, wept.

It only made Entrée's customers celebrate louder.

"Molly."

Molly turned her face into her pillow. It must have been her dreams calling her back, and she was more than willing to follow them. She reached out for a warm hand and clasped it tight. "Mmm," she murmured, sliding her fingers up an arm. So warm, so strong, powerful enough to lure her into its intimate dream embrace. She pressed the hand to her cheek.

"Molly?"

Molly bolted awake with a gasp. Then she gasped again at the sight of shirtless Adam in her bedroom. Then she gasped a third time as she flung his hand back at him so abruptly that he pounded himself on the chest. "What? What time is it?"

"It's nine-thirty. And ouch, by the way." He rubbed at his torso.

"Nine-thirty?" She threw back the covers and tried to leap out of bed but her fatigue and her weight kept her butt on the mattress. "It's late."

"Late for what?"

"Late for getting up."

"It's Sunday."

"Yeah, and—?"

Adam scratched his head, his blond hair sticking out in different sleepy directions. "You have a phone call."

"You answered my phone?"

"It was ringing, and I thought it was the logical thing to do to make it stop. Besides, I don't think I can ignore your ringing phone for a whole year."

He handed her the cordless receiver and retreated from the room. He was only wearing boxer shorts, and his legs were—his taut, muscular, long legs—well, there they were.

She was grateful that he'd seen fit to mute the phone, so her caller hadn't heard the barely civil exchange. She unmuted it and cleared her throat. "Hello?"

"Hey, Molly, it's Rebecca."

"Hi." Molly cradled the phone on one shoulder as she turned a pillow vertical and leaned back on it.

"New secretary?"

"Uh, yeah." She twisted her lips, embarrassed. "He might not work out though."

"Anything new?"

"Nope," Molly answered, trying to sound light and casual and normal. "How about you?"

"Let me rephrase," Rebecca said. "Is there anything you might want to tell me?"

"Anything specific you had in mind?" Molly countered.

"Well, only that an adorable couple got engaged at a front table in Entrée last night. And the woman, who happened to be pregnant, apparently had very similar facial features to, well, you."

Molly clapped a hand to her forehead.

"But I thought," Rebecca went on, "no way, because I had just spent about two hours with you at lunchtime yesterday and you didn't even breathe a word about a boyfriend."

"Um—"

"So, the missing piece of the puzzle must be that you have an evil twin running around pretending to be you. I just thought I'd let you know, in case she started trying to buy DVD players with your credit card or something."

Molly sighed. "Marti told you."

"No, actually, it was Rhonda."

"Rhonda wasn't there!" Or was she? Rhonda, that rattlesnake. She must have been coiled up and camouflaged somewhere in the restaurant. Maybe behind the big stone fireplace.

"Oh, yes she was. She said the man got down on one knee."

Molly sighed hard.

"And," Rebecca continued, "she said that from where she was sitting—and these are her words and not mine—she could tell he had a great butt."

"I will beat that woman to a dripping, bloody pulp when I see her again."

"Hey, I'm all for that. But first things first. Is it the guy who answered the phone, and was it really you, and are you engaged, and what in the world is going *on,* woman?"

"The guy is Adam Shibbs. The woman was me. We are engaged. And so—we're getting married."

Rebecca shrieked. "When did you meet him, like twenty minutes ago?"

"More like about fourteen years ago. In college."

"Your college sweetheart? That's romantic."

"No, he was my best friend then. But, I mean, he's still my best friend now. I just—we, well—"

"It suddenly turned into something more?"

Molly thought it over. "That's a very accurate way to put it."

After deflecting her friend's curious, well-intentioned questions about setting a wedding date and various other new-bride inquiries, Molly padded in her socks into the living room to replace the phone on the charger. Adam lay sprawled on his back across the fold-out, his long limbs taking up a lot more bed space than Molly would have thought, had she thought about it at all. The blue sheet she'd given him was twisted around the bottom half of his torso and also around one of his ankles. His arm was thrown over his eyes, giving her a perfect view of the inside of his bicep, and the soft thin skin covering the hard muscle.

She tried not to look. What was there to see, after

all? She'd been looking at Adam for nearly a decade and a half.

But, a little mischievous voice singsonged in her head, you haven't seen him like this. Sleeping in her living room as a semipermanent housemate. As her nearly naked fiancé.

"Everything all right?" she heard, and she realized he'd spoken without moving. She tightened her robe around herself. Her nipples had tightened and were poking through her thin nightshirt like twin troublemakers. That settled it. She was turning on the heat in this house. She didn't care if tomorrow was only Labor Day.

"No, not all right," Molly said. "The entire town knows we're engaged. Turns out the town blabbermouth was at Entrée last night."

"Excellent," Adam said, barely moving his lips. "Saves us the trouble of spreading the rumor ourselves."

"That's not funny."

"I'm one hundred percent serious," he said, still motionless. "The seed has been planted. The elaborate ruse has begun. Let someone else do our dirty work for us."

"No," Molly said, beginning to pace around the fold-out bed. "If it's uncontrolled gossip, we can't spin it to our advantage."

"Why should we have to? The only thing we don't want anyone to find out is that we did this to get and keep you a job assignment. And not even the most creative gossipmonger will be able to come up with that. Anything else they want to say about us, I don't care."

Molly reached the wall, completing her half circle around the fold-out. She turned to pace in the other direction. "I don't know," she muttered. "I just don't know about this whole thing."

"It's too late. When's your interview, anyhow?"

"Friday afternoon."

"Great. We'll go to the justice of the peace this week and do the deed."

"I can't." But as soon as the words left her mouth, she regretted them. *I can't lose my nerve. I can't back down now. I can't veer off the plan, a good plan, a crazy but solid plan.* "What I mean is, I can't—I can't take another day off from work this week. Tomorrow's Labor Day, Friday I have to go in to Manhattan for the interview, and the three days in between I have meetings with clients and way too much work to do for a three-day week."

"Fine. We'll get married Friday morning, then shoot you down to Manhattan in my car."

"Are you serious?" She raised her hand to brush a lock of hair out of her face, and the diamond glinted right into her eye. It mesmerized her for a moment, the way diamonds had been mesmerizing women for centuries. "You are serious. Right. So am I. Great. Friday it is."

"My mom and Janine are coming."

Molly had an urge to argue but realized she had no real desire to. Adam's family was—well, good to have around. "My parents aren't," she said instead.

"Are you even going to tell them?"

"Why should I? They're on the opposite side of the country. They'll never know. They probably won't even visit this year. They were here last year."

She said that with zero bitterness. Her parents were a CEO and a CFO. They were beyond busy. That, she had no problem understanding. Anyway, she wasn't needy, fragile or dependent. She had her own life, strange as it had quickly become.

"Ah," Adam said.

Molly kept pacing.

"You're kicking up a breeze," Adam finally said. "Could you stand still?"

Molly hadn't realized she was practically running back and forth. She halted, and panted a little bit.

"So, good. Wedding date set," Adam said. "Now we've got some organization."

At his last word, one of Molly's favorite words in the entire English language, the edges of her anxiety softened a little. Yes, things were getting organized, scheduled.

She looked at Adam again, who hadn't moved a muscle for this entire dialogue, except for the few around his mouth. She raised her hand and studied the ring again, a modest but perfect emerald-cut stone that was a miraculous perfect fit. "Aren't you worried about how this is going to totally redefine our friendship?" she finally asked.

Adam didn't answer for a long moment. "Should I?"

"We'll be married. *Spouses.* Living in the same house. Not to mention denying ourselves sex for a year."

"Well, why don't we just skip the last one? No sense piling on more pressure."

"Adam, you can*not* have sex with anyone. I mean, we're supposed to be married. I know you like—well, I know you like women." They liked him, too, Molly thought. So much that even though he wouldn't commit to anyone for any significant period of time, none of them bothered to hold it against him. Unreal. "And I like men," she added. Although the way Zach had treated her had made her reconsider that opinion for a while. Zach had been a shimmering golden dream of perfection, the man she always wanted, and after only forty-eight hours, she'd discovered he'd been nothing but an elaborate mirage. The only truly admirable thing about him had turned out to be his ambitious sperm.

"I'm glad to hear you like men, but, Molly, I *can* keep a marriage vow. Even to you."

"Hey!"

"And anyhow, I thought you were talking about sex with you and me."

What?

He still hadn't shifted a limb out of place. He

didn't think this through, Molly thought. He couldn't have. If he did, shouldn't this feel as difficult for him as it did for her?

Best to address this the way she did everything else. Head-on.

"We will never talk about sex with you and me. There can be no sex with you and me," she said, willing her tone to be authoritarian and unquestioned. "None. We're stretching our relationship to its logical limit already. It will not be able to withstand any more." She ran her gaze over all his bare skin and actually shivered. "I can't do a year of…of…sexual tension."

He mumbled something. It sounded like, "Neither can I," but she wasn't sure. She didn't get a chance to ask him to repeat himself, because he then said, louder, "If you're not going to have sex with me, then how about not staring at my very manly body while I'm trying to sleep?"

Molly felt herself grow hot, then picked up a sofa pillow that had ended up on the floor last night and threw it at him. Hard. He absorbed its crash into his chest by curling his body up, and Molly got a satisfaction out of finally forcing him into motion. "Then why don't you put some clothes on?" she asked.

He tossed the pillow in counterattack, but with far less force and purposefully bad aim. It landed four feet away from her. "I put on boxers," he said, "and purely for your benefit, I might add. I usually sleep naked."

Molly flounced out of the room. Or, more like

bounced. The baby, who'd managed to change so many things in her life already, was even affecting her ability to make a dramatic exit.

Adam, grateful for the twisted sheets obscuring particular body parts, fell back onto the still-warm pillows and remained lying there after Molly had stomped out. He knew that slipping back into sleep was an impossibility.

He'd stayed motionless throughout their entire charged conversation, because he couldn't trust his own reactions if he sat up and gazed at her straight on while she'd laid down the no-sex, no-how law.

Last night had been hard. Unexpectedly, and literally, in every sense. It shouldn't have been. He'd slept in Molly's former apartments before, just as she'd slept in his. After late evenings out, when one of them had one drink too many to responsibly drive home, they'd had no qualms about crashing out on the other's sofa, fully dressed, only to blow out the door early the next morning with a hurried but not entirely awkward thanks.

Last night was different. In the blackness of her living room, his eyes traced the unfamiliar outlines of her mostly new furniture. As minutes became an hour, he could swear the reason that slumber eluded him was because he could smell Molly's lily scent on the sheets, in the air, forming a beckoning trail to her bedroom. And after getting up to cool his sweating skin at the open window for the third time, he'd crept up the stairs. Just to check on her, of course. Not that anything could really happen to her in her own bed, which was where she was, deep in sleep. A little night-light in her small adjoining bathroom spilled the tiniest bit of brightness across the bed. Darkness obscured her face but the light caught the ring on her hand, resting on her pillow. Her arms and legs lay relaxed, calm, and nothing like her wound-tight, tense, daylight self. Her lips were parted, and Adam's own mouth went dry. He turned and went back downstairs.

Yes, last night *was* different and Adam feared it set the tone for 364 nights to come.

He reminded himself now that this was Molly, who didn't need a man like him just as much as he didn't need a woman like her. The internal memo should have reassured him.

He'd thought he could do this. He'd said he would do this. He *would* do this.

However, if he didn't get some sleep, he wouldn't be able to do anything. He flung his arm back over his face and closed his eyes, willing himself into at least one short nap, but a voice, a female voice that floated uncomfortably close, called, "Yoo-hoo! Molly? Are you home, sweetheart?"

Adam, startled, shot to his feet. He looked around for his jeans and as the calling voice got closer, he yanked the top sheet off the bed. Not realizing a piece of it was still wrapped around his leg, he proceeded to effectively trip himself into a sprawl on the hardwood floor. He put his hands on the floor to right himself and found himself looking at a pair of white orthopedic shoes. Slowly he raised his head to find an elderly woman holding a Pyrex dish.

"Oh, hello there, dear," the woman said, examining him from head to toe.

If he were actually standing, this very short, stout woman would have to crane her neck at quite an angle to carry on a conversation with him. Her silvery hair was puffed up and appeared solid enough to sustain minimal damage from a hurricane-force gale. Her makeup was careful but obvious, emphasizing eyes that were at once shrewd and amused. Adam instantly wanted to be on her side in any situation.

As Molly was nowhere to be found, and as the sight of a mostly naked man didn't seem to surprise this mystery lady, there remained a silence that it was Adam's onus to fill. So he cleared his throat, and asked the only question he could think of. "Are those brownies?"

Chapter Five

When Molly descended the stairs, she found her new fiancé and her next-door neighbor sharing brownies and laughs in her kitchen.

"Molly!" Sylvia Fulton cried, rising and enveloping Molly in her warm embrace. Molly tried to catch Adam's eye but he was too busy pouring himself a refill of milk.

"I didn't hear you come in," Molly apologized.

"That's fine, dear. I had heard that you got engaged last night, and I brought you some brownies to celebrate, but I had no idea that I would get to meet the man of the hour himself."

Molly, remembering that when she'd last seen

Adam, he'd been prone and tangled in the covers, felt herself turning red. Sylvia had doubtless also seen Adam in the guest bed. Anyone, even someone at Sylvia's senior age, would assume a woman wouldn't banish the man she loved to the sofa.

Molly couldn't believe their bad luck. They hadn't even been able to keep up the charade for twenty-four hours....

"I hope you didn't mind that I let myself in," Sylvia said. "You're usually up and around way earlier than this."

"I know," Molly said, her voice fading a little. "Uh, Sylvia..."

"Don't be embarrassed, sweetheart," Sylvia said. "Adam explained to me why he was sleeping downstairs, and I won't tell a soul."

It was true that Sylvia wasn't a gossip, but Molly would have liked to know just what it was she wouldn't be gossiping about. "I see," she said carefully. "So, Adam told you that—that thing?"

"I deeply respect your decision," Sylvia said, leading Molly to the table and helping her sit as if it was Molly who were the guest in her own kitchen. She took a teapot off the stove, filled a cup and placed it in front of Molly. Molly tried to catch Adam's eye again, but he was lifting another brownie from the dish. This time, it was obvious he was avoiding her questioning look. At least he'd put on a pair of jeans and an ancient AC/DC T-shirt.

"Waiting until you're married is a wonderful decision," Sylvia continued, sitting down between them. "That's what Horace and I did. And, well, we almost made it."

Molly breathed in too hard around a mouthful of tea and turned from the table, coughing hard. When she turned back, she caught Adam's grin before he hid it by lifting his glass to his face.

"Are you all right?" Sylvia asked.

Molly nodded.

"Anyway, it's very romantic," Sylvia said. "And old-fashioned. A whirlwind romance and all."

Molly looked down at her belly. "I wouldn't call it old-fashioned, or traditional, considering the sequence of events."

Sylvia smiled. "How could you know when you decided to have a baby on your own that Adam was right around the corner?" She patted Molly's hand. "Things always unfold in the order they're supposed to, not in the order we expect them to. It's your destiny."

At the same time that Molly felt a twinge of guilt at deceiving this woman, this grandmotherly friend, she so desperately wanted to believe the prophetic words. She hadn't planned any of the last six months, and her life had spiraled frustratingly out of her control. Zach, her baby, getting fired, Adam—was it just the right sequence of events to get her where she needed to be? Where did she need to be?

"So," Sylvia said, handing Molly a gooey, still-warm brownie, "when's the big day?"

"As soon as possible," Adam told her honestly. "We can't wait."

Sylvia laughed. "I can't blame you. After all, that night, that's what I finally told Horace."

Why I'm Not Going to Last a Year with Adam Shibbs:

1. He watches too much TV.
2. He insists on being social with every single neighbor.
3. He brought a puppy with ADHD to live in my house.

Molly threw down her pen. She was feeling a stab of guilt, and why should she? Every item on this list so far was true.

She went back over the items. Number one. Adam did watch too much TV. Okay, maybe just one or two cartoons for the most part, but on Labor Day, they had nothing planned, so Adam plopped himself down in front of the tube for a Mets game, a *Welcome Back, Kotter* marathon, a program on diamondback snakes, an Italian cooking show that he took notes on, a colorful variety show on the Spanish station—he claimed to know enough Spanish to follow it—*The Situation Room* and a special two-hour presentation on shipwrecks.

He had repeatedly invited Molly to sit and watch, but she'd informed him some people had serious lives to lead. He'd insisted he could learn more from an occasional long day of TV than a semester in college. Molly didn't know about that, but she had sat at the top of the stairs, where he couldn't see her, and listened to the snake show. Only because it was *kind* of interesting. But she hid because she hadn't wanted Adam to think he could turn her into a layabout. She'd gotten a cramp in her right leg from the way she'd crouched on the step.

She rubbed her calf now as she looked at bullet point number two. Despite the fact that Molly had been trying to keep them low-key, Adam just could not help making friends with the entire block. Tuesday evening, after work, he vanished for two hours and told Molly later he had attended the yoga class Sylvia taught at the senior citizen center. Apparently, the older woman thought his presence would encourage more over-65 ladies to join.

And it was as if he was telling the world about their engagement.

On Wednesday, Molly had seen him chatting to Rebecca outside for ten full minutes about who knew what, and whatever it was made him give her a friendly hug. Which Molly didn't care about. Because she wasn't jealous or anything. But it was bad enough they were lying to the neighborhood. Did he have to become big buddies with everyone also?

Elmer, now lying at his new mistress's feet, whined and Molly rubbed him between his floppy ears. She'd tried to convince Adam to leave Elmer with Janine and the boys, but Adam had refused, saying he was Elmer's parent. When the puppy had first entered Molly's house, he scrambled over to her at top speed and leaped on her, licking her entire face.

And all right, he was cute. In fact, really cute, and wiggly and soft, and Molly really liked him. But the point was, Adam didn't know she would. So he shouldn't have just assumed she would.

Even though she did. "Good boy, Elmer," she murmured.

Oh, God, she was marrying Adam tomorrow.

She crumpled and twisted up her list and threw it in the trash.

She held up her hand, moving her fingers so the diamond sparkled under her desk lamp. Elmer licked her palm.

Adam checked his wrist and, for the fourth time in a row, found nothing but a freckle. If he'd been the sort of man to wear a watch, it would have yielded him some concrete information. Instead, he had only his powers of estimation and, according to those, Molly had kept him waiting in the Rosewood Town Hall corridor for close to a half hour.

He leaned one shoulder against the wall and shoved his hand in his pocket in search of loose change to jingle. He found none, which made sense seeing as he hadn't worn this suit since—well, it had been a long while. He crossed his arms, then put his hands on his hips, then stood up straight and let his arms dangle at his sides.

The open door at the end of the hallway was the meeting room where the justice of the peace had arranged the ceremony to take place. Adam's female family members had arrived a little while ago, his mother holding a wide, fragrant rainbow of a bouquet for Molly, and Janine lugging a mysterious black canvas bag.

Molly had been shown to a small unoccupied office to "get ready." Adam wasn't sure what kind of getting ready could be going on in there for so long, unless there was a secret full-spa-treatment, hair-and-makeup facility and three masseuses in the room. He wished Molly would at least send one of them out. He could use a good neck rub.

Giving up on that scenario, Adam began to wonder if Molly had escaped out a window, à la classic runaway bride. Sure, they were on the second floor, but not much could stop Molly. She could've easily knotted a rope ladder out of her pantyhose or something.

At this point, he half expected that prospect would relieve him with a definite way out. Instead, the thought of Molly shimmying down the beige brick wall and scurrying across the parking lot made him break out in a chilling perspiration. He tugged at his nooselike tie.

He was fighting the urge to kick the door into splinters and survey the situation when Janine and his mother *click-clacked* in their high heels down the hall.

"Where's the bride?" Pam asked.

"That's what I'd like to know."

His own mouth forming the insecure complaint felt really wrong.

His mother said nothing for a moment, then laid a hand on her son's arm. "If I know that girl, she needs to be zipped into her skirt or something, and she's just too proud to ask for help. I'll go check on her."

She pressed her ear against the door and rapped twice, lightly. Adam didn't hear Molly's invitation from within but maybe his mother did, because she slid in quietly and closed the door behind her.

Adam let out a breath he hadn't known he was holding tight inside the constrictive casing of his lungs. His mom would take care of whatever was going on. She'd been taking charge for many years, and it was impossible to overestimate her abilities.

Adam stood with his sister in silence for a few moments.

"I must say," Janine said, "this is a very convenient site you've chosen for your nuptials. I just might pay an overdue ticket before we leave." She nodded her chin toward the office of the parking clerk.

Adam recognized her attempt at a joke, but he didn't have the sharpness of mind to try to top it.

"That room down there is nice and quiet, though,"

Janine continued. "Mom and I brought a few candles so we could turn down the predictable florescent lighting. And to complete the perfect romantic ambiance, I even brought my portable keyboard for some music."

Adam saw a weak opening. "You really think Molly's going to want to walk down the aisle to 'Jingle Bells'?"

"I've learned a few other songs since then, I'll have you know. 'Row, Row Your Boat' and 'Frère Jacques' are both big hits at parties. But I was considering the decidedly less ambitious 'Canon in D' by Pachelbel."

Adam raised an eyebrow.

"There, you see?" she said. "You're not the only Shibbs with a few surprises up the sleeve."

"I never doubted you for a minute."

"And I don't doubt you." She studied his face. "And as hard as you work to maintain the facade, I know for a fact that you're no fool. I have a good feeling about all of this." She paused. "Whatever this is."

"Then give up a hug," Adam said, "and pass on a little bit of that feeling."

Janine wrapped her arms around his waist. "Ew, you're all sweaty." She squeezed. "You're quite a brother," she said into his chest. "And from what I can tell, you're quite a friend, too."

"I hope I at least have *that* left when this is—" *All over,* he thought. *When I'm single again.*

Would he and Molly be what they were, or would

their friendship, the relationship he valued most in his life full of friends and fun, be the biggest casualty of the inevitable divorce?

Janine waited for the end of his sentence, but he didn't offer it, and she didn't press for it. She dropped her arms, smiled and turned to walk back down the corridor. "Thanks for the sister-in-law, by the way," she said over her shoulder. "Two against one are much more palatable odds."

Adam waited until she disappeared into the meeting room, then crossed the hall in two long steps. He was about to press his ear to the door like his mother had when he realized the door hadn't actually caught. He nudged it open an extra inch with one finger, slowly, willing it not to creak and give him away.

Snooping wasn't cool, but the suspense was close to killing him.

"I love my son very much," he heard his mother say.

A long time passed with no response from the bride. Adam realized he was waiting for her to echo the sentiment, and then realized that that would be like waiting in the rain for a broken-down bus. Of course Molly couldn't say she loved him.

But Molly said something then, so quiet Adam didn't catch the words. He cursed to himself and tried to squint with his ears.

"I know you know," his mother answered. "And for the record, I love you also. And that love includes the trust that this is going to turn out all right for both my son and for you. I can't tell two adults how to live your lives, but as long as no one is hurt in any way, I can stand aside with a clear conscience and watch you two do whatever it is you have to do."

This time, Molly was a bit louder. "Thank you."

He heard his mother sigh. "Adam is—well, you know how Adam is."

"He's the anti-me."

Adam started to chuckle, then stopped himself from doing it so as not to give away his stealth position.

"But, it's odd," Pam went on. "He might be the anti-you, but over the years, I have noticed this—that you somehow make him smile more than anything else he has or does."

Adam edged the door a little wider to hear Molly's response, which emanated at just above a whisper. "Really?"

Pam laughed—that low, deep laugh that mothers let out when the children in their lives discover something obvious. "I have a feeling you meant that as a rhetorical question, but I believe it does have an answer. Maybe now you and Adam will get closer to it."

The sound of heels approached the door, and Adam leaped back and landed like a surefooted panther at the original spot where his mother had left him. But then he heard Pam again, nearer to the open door.

"Oh, I almost forgot. Janine wanted to make sure you got your something old. Here it is. It's a picture of Adam as a baby."

Molly laughed. "That's so cute! He's totally covered in soapsuds."

Janine, that fink. It was the photo of him in the bathtub with his little red boat. Adam vowed to get back at his sister at the very earliest opportunity.

"She says if you're going to be a Shibbs, you need to have a stash of blackmail material," Pam said. "Just slip it in your purse for something old. And you've got your something new in your belly there, haven't you? Put on my sapphire earrings for your something blue. And you need something borrowed…."

"I do have that," Molly said.

"Then the last thing you need is a handkerchief. Wouldn't want tears to ruin your makeup."

"I'm not going to cry."

"Well, just in case you spill something, then."

"Thank you."

Pam opened the door and Adam stared up at the ceiling tiles, putting on a show of being lost in thought. Then he looked at his mother and did an elaborate double take. "Oh, there you are. Everything all right?"

"As if you don't know, Double-O-Seven," his mother retorted. "I expect to see you down the hall shortly. Don't keep three women waiting." She touched his cheek and walked away.

Without thinking about it, Adam pushed open the door and walked in on Molly—who was dabbing her eyes with the handkerchief.

Adam didn't say anything, but he did close the door behind him. Molly turned her back to him, and Adam interpreted that as her not wanting questions.

He heard a few sniffles, and eventually she stuffed the handkerchief into her little beaded purse. Then she turned back around. Her nose was red.

"I do hope you're not thinking of backing out, Shibbs. I happen to have in my possession a very incriminating naked photo of you." She held up the picture, curled at the edges by time. "I don't want to have to go to the tabloids."

Adam was touched by her attempt to cut through the tension with humor. "You drive a hard bargain, Moll."

"I always do."

"Well, then, do I have a deal for you." He felt hot. He instinctively glanced at the wall to see outside, to steady himself, but there were no windows in here. There was an open closet, and on the inside of the door was a mirror. He could see his own face and it seemed like the face of someone he'd never met. A nervous, stammering, flushed stranger.

"A deal?" Molly inquired.

He tore his eyes away from his own image and faced Molly. "Yes, I'd like to kiss the bride."

He'd surprised her, but she recovered quickly. "I do expect it to be part of the ceremony."

"I mean, let's do it now."

"What?"

"Molly," he said, an urgency rising from his core,

"the justice of the peace is going to kick us out for dawdling his day away. Just stand still and let me kiss you now."

"But—"

"I don't want our first kiss to be in front of an audience. Even a small select audience. It wouldn't—it won't be right."

Molly inhaled and, assuming a protest was forthcoming, Adam added, "Besides, it will take the pressure off the actual moment, right?"

Molly stilled. "Well, all—all right, I guess. Yes."

Adam stepped over to his friend—his bride. He lifted his hands and brushed her hair off her shoulders.

He'd dated a lot of women. He'd kissed the majority of them, at the very least. But he hadn't had any idea that he'd compared any of them to Molly until this moment, when he had the real Molly standing before him and his mind defaulted into error mode, unable to make its usual comparison.

He was in big, big trouble here.

At the last second before his lips touched hers, her eyes fluttered closed, and a faint freckle on one soft, thin eyelid was the last thing he saw before his own shut, as well.

When Adam was a kid, someone once gave him a handful of red candies, which Adam popped immediately into his mouth, expecting a cherry flavor. Then he saw his friend grin with sadistic satisfaction, and before he could stop it from happening, the red-hot cinnamon candies burned into his tongue, into the delicate skin at the roof of his mouth. It was an extreme taste that he was sure would permanently sear his taste buds, so that for years to follow, whenever he ate hamburgers, chocolate ice cream, spaghetti and meatballs, he would always taste the cinnamon there, too.

That cinnamon had faded after all. But the taste of Molly's lips—new but familiar, exotic but full of contentment—was stronger, more powerful and much more permanent.

He pulled back, and her bottom lip lingered on his a microsecond too long, as if she didn't want him to go.

They stared at each other for an electrified minute.

"By the way," he finally said, and the words came out hoarse and parched, "what's borrowed?"

"What?" She sounded just as ragged.

"I heard you say you already had your something borrowed, but you didn't say what it is."

She put two fingers to her lips and touched them in a soft caress, as if to lift the imprint of their kiss. "It's you," she said.

A shudder hovered in his bones, threatening to shake him until he fell to the floor, but he fought it with all his strength. He squared his shoulders. "I think—I think it's showtime."

"I think—I'll meet you out there."

Molly put one foot in front of the other, beginning her lone trek down the aisle. Nobody was beside her, cradling her arm to give her away, but it was just as well, because no one would have been qualified to claim she was theirs to give away. She far preferred to make the short but intimidating trip on her own.

Besides, if for some reason she'd been forced to choose someone to walk with her, she probably would have picked Adam, to crack jokes and coax out her smile at the most nerve-racking moment of her life.

And as it was, Adam was there. But he was way at the other end of the aisle, standing in the spot designated for the person she was giving herself away to.

It was no surprise that he was wearing the charcoal suit, or that his dress shoes were freshly shined with black polish. Eschewing wedding-day superstition, she'd been in his sight all morning. She'd eaten breakfast with him, drove to town hall with him. But they hadn't said much.

What could she have said that would have eased their trepidation? What could he have said?

Every shaky step brought her a few inches closer to Adam, who shouldn't ever seem unfamiliar in any way, but somehow he did now. He appeared to be standing taller than his six-foot height, and his ever-present grin-at-the-world was gone. He was serious, solid, reliable and immovable.

Or did she just want him to be?

Oh, Adam…

She couldn't look at him anymore, because it scared the hell out of her that he suddenly looked like what she'd always wanted. She fought the urge to bend over, yank off the exquisite cream-colored shoes and fling them over her shoulder as she fled out into the midmorning sunshine.

Stick to the plan, Molly Jackson. A good plan. A crazy but solid plan.

She refocused her attention, this time on the man standing beside Adam. The justice of the peace was a middle-aged, pleasant man who, upon meeting her, hadn't blinked or raised an eyebrow at her obviously delicate state. He's witnessed this before, Molly realized now. I'm nothing new.

Halfway down the short aisle and moving at a glacial pace in spite of her racing thoughts, she turned her head from right to left, surveying the nearly empty, bland meeting room. There was only one small window, but it was shut and the light from several candles flickered and danced across the drawn blinds.

Suddenly, her mind multiplied the few chairs into dozens and dozens, all occupied by unrecognizable women. More women stood lining the entire perimeter of the room, and the air around Molly warmed to golden at the presence of so many unexpected guests. All ages, all sizes, all smiling at the awkward bride, welcoming her into their midst. They nodded their ghostly approval and encouragement at the new one to join their ranks, another woman who, by choice or by necessity, was living her life outside of society's usual order.

And in this transformed room, Molly's fear of not doing things right, in their sensible, predetermined sequence, dissipated. The collective power of her predecessors propelled her forward, faster, gave her the strength to take Adam's hand, and finally to meet his gaze.

When he smiled down at her, the paranormal audience faded, no longer needed, but the warmth remained. The residual heat of Adam's brief kiss was still itchy and hot on her lips, like a new, barely completed tattoo.

She hadn't noticed the pretty melody Janine was playing until its last quiet notes echoed away, leaving them all in a subtle silence.

It occurred to Molly that if she'd told Adam about the presence she'd experienced, the women she'd conjured, he would have believed her. And it wouldn't be strange to her if maybe he had seen them, too.

But she didn't tell him. Instead, she whispered, "I do" with conviction, even though it was just a few minutes too early to say it.

Chapter Six

"I do," Molly said, "have an extensive list of references for you, Mr. Tilberg."

She opened up her black leather folder and slid out a list that took up an entire side—single-spaced—of a sheet of ivory stock. She was proud of every printed word that formed this list.

Now, all she had to do was make sure it met *this* man's approval.

Pieter Tilberg took the paper from her, glanced at it, and made some kind of notation with his red pen in the top margin. He had short, white-blond hair and he had none of the thickness around his midsection that middle age usually brought along when it arrived.

He'd stood at an impressive height when he'd entered the room, and her first thought was that if she'd seen him outside, from across-the-street distance, she would have assumed he was an SUNY student grabbing a burger between classes. But here, with only the polished meeting table between them in the midtown hotel suite, she was close enough to see the subtle silvery hairs hidden among pale blond, and the deep groove cutting through the center of his forehead and hitting the bridge of his thin wire glasses.

He placed her reference list in a manila folder in front of him, for later scrutiny.

Molly folded her hands in her lap, marveling at her own calm only a few hours after the morning's emotional carnival ride. This—this was her place, where she belonged. Two of Tilberg's ALCOP associates had grilled her for nearly an hour on her qualifications, tossing out hypothetical situations for Molly to handle. By the end of their inquisition, all three were smiling and jovial, silently acknowledging that she was a perfect fit. But then the men said the ALCOP president, Pieter Tilberg, liked to have a few minutes alone with each candidate, and the look the two men gave her before leaving her seemed suspiciously like pity.

Then Tilberg had entered and sat down in a seat one of his associates had vacated, but the chair seemed too small to contain his presence.

But she was good at this, too, Molly reminded herself—extolling her numerous professional virtues to an intimidating, influential person. As long as she managed not to think about what hung in the balance for her this time around. She felt one pinky trembling, but she held it down with her ring finger on the other hand. The finger with two new rings. She didn't think Pieter Tilberg noticed.

He seemed to want to look everywhere but at her, which was less than a positive sign. Usually by this point in an interview with a potential client, the interviewer would be regarding Molly with an expression of admiration and relief at having finally found the person qualified to treat whatever illness ailed his or her company. But Tilberg's gaze ran through her like glass to the wallpaper behind her.

Molly tried not to panic at how much more this was going to require. She'd expected it, and was prepared for it, but when it came right down to it, she'd still walked in here hoping the industry rumors about Tilberg hadn't been true.

"I also have," she said, slipping her hand into her portfolio again, "in addition to the plan I've drawn up for your anticipated implementation needs, a post-pregnancy work schedule."

Tilberg flicked his eye onto the next piece of paper she handed him but then looked at her again, this time right into her eyes. "What's this for?" he asked, and his confusion sounded sincere.

"I'm sure it hasn't escaped your attention that I'm pregnant."

"Well, I am surprised at your addressing the issue so, let's say, frankly," he said.

He hadn't strung together that many words at one time for her yet in this short meeting, and his accent, not very noticeable in his previous two- and three-word sentences, emerged distinctly. Any hint of emotion, however, was still lacking on his end, so that instead of sounding like a robot, he now sounded like a robot manufactured overseas.

"I understand this is not the kind of thing an employer discusses in an interview," he continued. "It is not supposed to influence my decision."

Molly was not naive enough to be fooled by his assurance. She wanted the upper hand here. "You're not bringing it up. I am. I prefer to discuss it," Molly said. "I drew up that plan so you could see how not only will I be devoting as much time to ALCOP as before having my baby, I'll actually have more time for you because I am nearing the completion of a long project for another client."

"This is impressive," Tilberg said, though Molly couldn't confirm the validity of that statement when delivered in a monotone. "You must have good day care?"

"My—my husband, Adam, will be taking some time off," Molly said. She tried not to grind her back teeth to stubs at having to say this to a potential boss, but on the other hand, she had married Adam so that she would be able to say this when the opportunity arose. There, now it was said.

And why had she kissed Adam? What did she stand to gain from it? It wasn't as if she were going to have any occasion to say *that* in an interview.

Hey, Mr. Tilberg, incidentally, I kissed Adam. Right, he is my husband. But he's only my husband since this morning. The kiss? Well, it was...it was...short. But I wanted it to be longer. Oh, no, did I? I couldn't have. But I felt...I felt...

"Very fortunate."

His words blinked Molly out of her brief but unprofessional reverie. Luckily, Tilberg was examining her printout and, once again, ignoring her. A bald eagle could smash through the picture window facing the Empire State Building, land on her shoulder and sing "The Star-Spangled Banner" and Tilberg wouldn't bat an eyelash.

"Thank you, but I don't consider it fortunate that my husband is helping me," she said with a smile. "It's deliberate. I would not have chosen a partner who I couldn't work with."

"Interesting."

Okay, pal, that's it, Molly thought. *You have no idea what I've gone through for this job, what I've gone through so I can work for you. Isn't that enough? What the hell else do I have to do, to say, to impress you?*

The silence stretched between them, potentially discomfiting for a lesser job candidate, but if Tilberg thought he could unsettle Molly into leaving, he was wrong.

"I want this job," she said, injecting into her words the respect that she didn't feel. Then she stopped speaking. This time, the silence was hers to control. Only when he tilted his chin up and looked her in the eye again did she continue. "I want this job because I know that out of all the candidates you'll interview, I'll do the best work and get the most results for you."

"That's confidence," he commented.

"That it is," Molly said. "To be blunt, Mr. Tilberg, *I'm your man.*"

Had she meant to say that?

Tilberg sat back and blinked, and then one tight corner of his mouth twitched. It didn't turn into a smile, or a frown, or anything indicative of his opinion of her, but that small signal was enough for Molly to know he was at least *having* an opinion.

Well, yeah, she had meant to say that.

"Ah," he said finally, and Molly breathed in the deep satisfaction that that one syllable gave her.

After she shook Tilberg's hand and left the room, she walked away knowing she'd done everything in her power to make a strong impression. If she didn't get the job, it was something insurmountable, something that wasn't her fault, something that had to do with Tilberg himself that no one could possibly change.

But, good reasons aside, if she didn't get the job, what in the hell would she do for money?

Adam, double-parked across the street in a slightly

different spot than before—suggesting he'd been shooed off by a meter maid, possibly more than once—waved out the passenger-side window and she darted across the street, clutching her portfolio. She hopped into the car, the fully blasting air-conditioning blowing her hair back and cooling her earlobes.

"It went great?" Adam asked.

"As great as it could, considering that guy," Molly answered.

"Terrific. Late lunch to celebrate?"

"I don't know yet if there's a cause for celebration."

"Come on. If I just married me, I'd be celebrating. And we've still got the wedding night to look forward to."

Her heart stopped in her chest, and she tried to make it start again by taking a deep breath, but it felt as if the breath went nowhere. "We're not—I mean, you don't mean—" she stammered.

"I mean a classic, tried-and-true, two-person activity."

"You mean—"

"Yup," he said. "Checkers."

Molly's breath caught in her throat, making a weird noise, and then she laughed. She laughed so hard, she thought her sides would break open. She put an arm around her middle to keep her baby inside while she kept laughing. When she could speak, she told him, "I'm really in the mood to win."

"So am I. Best two of three. And in the unlikely

event that I lose, I've now got a whole year of games to even the score."

Molly glanced out her window as a yellow cab nearly sideswiped them in its hurry to change lanes.

If she didn't get the job, what in the hell would she do with her new husband?

Adam hadn't unpacked his alarm clock yet, but he was discovering—the loud way—that any roommate of Molly's wouldn't need one. Her fingers slammed against her computer keyboard, heralding the crack of dawn like an overambitious Type-A rooster.

He sat up and rubbed his eyes. He could not believe how hard Molly, one staircase and several rooms away, hit those keys, and he couldn't imagine why she didn't have crippling carpal tunnel syndrome to go with her hunched-over shoulders and her failing eyesight. She'd had to put her reading glasses on to play checkers last night after losing one game to him. Of course, he should have disqualified her for it, because she then came back for a hard-fought two in a row to best him. He'd wanted to be annoyed at her victory dance, but her dark curls dancing around her head and the way she had to wrap an arm around the baby while she waved her other arm in the air was...well, it was cute. Even her little chant that went something like, "I won and you lost." It was endearing in a way that, as far as he knew, Molly rarely allowed herself to be.

Then they'd watched late-night stand-up comedy on TV, made microwave popcorn and took turns throwing kernels into each other's open mouths from opposite ends of the sofa. He'd tried not to think, aiming at her open mouth, that he now knew exactly how that mouth tasted. Better than popcorn. Better than anything, anyone.

Then, with the popcorn half-gone and a comedienne only a few jokes into her routine, Molly had suddenly leaped up, mumbled something about being tired and rushed upstairs, not to be heard from again.

Until this morning, when that manic typing began. And on a Saturday, no less.

Well, he was awake now, so he might as well start his own day. He rolled off the bed and began to straighten the sheets so he could fold it back into the sofa. Elmer sat at the bottom of the stairs, heavy tail thumping, his head cocked to one side, enthralled with Molly's racket.

"Moll!" Adam called, but she didn't hear him. He finished with the bed, took the stairs two at a time and headed to her office. The hallway was bright with morning sun coming in from every room, with one dark corner where the door to the "nursery" remained closed. Adam stopped for a moment and stared at the door, at its flawless white paint. This room was starting to creep him out a little bit. He didn't understand why Molly, who scheduled every sneeze into her day planner, hadn't even started decorating that room.

The rest of her house was so nurtured and pretty. He'd have assumed she'd be overly eager to get that room cheerily decorated, too. What was the deal?

He shook his head at the mystery and moved away to knock on her half-open office door. "Molly?"

The typing ceased. "What's wrong?"

"Nothing's wrong. I just got up. There hasn't been time for anything to go wrong."

"Then...what?"

"I'm taking Elmer out. Want to come?"

"Um, no...I have all this stuff to do."

"Okay. How about, after you're done, we'll walk him to the park and toss a ball around?"

"I'm not really going to be done..."

"Ever?"

"Well, after I finish up here, I have some work around the house."

"Which you should not be doing. How about taking it easy?"

"I'm taking it the way I want to take it," Molly said. "I'm a big girl. It's my choice."

"You're making a choice to spend all day Saturday working?"

"Yes. There are always things to do."

Her response was an echo of one he'd heard long ago.

"Dad, why do you have to go to work today? It's Saturday."

Dad smiled, but Adam knew full well it wasn't

real. It was just to make Adam feel better. His father wasn't a smiler. "Adam, work doesn't know what day it is. There are always things to do."

"You'll play catch with me later when you get home, right?"

"If it's not already dark out, champ."

"We just set the clocks back, remember? It won't get dark until I go to bed."

His dad's face looked the way Adam felt when he got his braces tightened. But his dad didn't have braces. "Well, I'll try," Dad said. "Sometimes, well, sometimes there just isn't enough time. Don't get your hopes up, okay?"

Adam didn't say anything, but Dad stood there until Adam said, "Okay." Dad walked quickly to the car, briefcase swinging. Adam felt bad for lying, but not for hoping his dad would get home before dark anyway.

Adam blinked. Sometimes there just isn't enough time. His dad had had no idea how little time he'd actually had. If he did, Adam had a feeling he would have seen a lot more of his father in those years—and for many more years. "Fine," Adam said. "All right. Maybe after dinner we can catch a flick."

"Listen, Adam," Molly said, swiveling her chair around to face him. "It's not that that doesn't sound like fun. But I have a baby coming. I suddenly have a husband, another person living in the same house as me. If much more about my lifestyle changes, I'll go insane. On a normal Saturday, I get stuff done.

Please don't ask me to change that, too. I need to keep some things normal. Okay?"

"Okay," Adam said, and he felt bad for lying, but not for hoping he could do something about—no, for—Molly.

A glimmer of an idea was forming in his mind. He moved toward the door. "I'm going to have fun today," he said, as if it were an afterthought.

"Good for you."

"So," he went on, "if you just happen to see me having fun, and you feel a crazy urge to join me in that fun, please do it."

"Um, sure," Molly said, but she'd already pushed her reading glasses up on her nose, stuck a pencil in the braided knot of hair at her neck and turned back to the computer screen.

Before Adam left the room, he crossed over to her window and opened the curtains wide, giving her a good view of her side lawn, if she was going to be bothered to check it out.

"What are you doing?" she mumbled.

"You need more light to read," he said, leaving and gently shutting the door. Then he quietly moved around the house, opening all the windows wide.

Every fifteen-hour day his father had spent working was a day closer to the heart attack he'd eventually induced. But Adam, only a teenager, hadn't been able to predict that, and he hadn't been able to stop his father, to change him.

The heartbreaking loss had nevertheless been an important part of life, a lesson learned. Adam was smarter now, and stronger. He'd designed his own life to be the opposite. Long—and happy. He'd always wanted Molly to have the same kind of long, happy life, and he felt it was his task to help secure it for her now that she was, well, now that they were—

They wouldn't be married for long, okay. But he still needed to do this for her. For him. No, for her.

Molly was going to see and hear fun everywhere, all day today. And, dammit, she was going to be part of that fun if it was the last thing he ever did.

From 10:00 a.m. to 11:00 a.m., Adam romped with Elmer in front of the house, wrestling with a thick stick, tossing a Frisbee, rolling in the grass.

When he peeked in the house, Molly was dusting the mantel with an orange rag.

From 11:00 a.m. until noon, he sat on a lawn chair in the backyard, eating a huge sandwich, drinking a root beer, listening to a Top 30 countdown on the radio and working through a book of Sudoku puzzles.

When he peeked in the house, Molly was sorting laundry into piles.

From noon to 2:00 p.m., he settled himself in front of the television and watched *Breakfast at Tiffany's* from beginning to end. This should have been a clincher. For crying out loud, didn't *all* women love this movie? He turned it up a bit more every time he heard Molly approaching the living room, but he didn't issue a verbal invitation. Instead, he tried to appear totally absorbed in the drama.

At 2:00 p.m., Adam made sure Molly *wasn't* nearby before he sniffed and swiped at his eyes. Stupid movie.

From 2:00 p.m. to 4:30 p.m., he organized an epic kickball game for some Danbury Way kids, and kids on neighboring streets who'd heard the shrieks and yelling and had come to investigate. He agreed to be the pitcher for both teams, and created rhyming cheers to boost the losing side. Elmer unwittingly played outfield, chasing the ball after any particularly powerful kick sent it up the street.

At 4:30 p.m., Adam left amid happy cries of "'Bye, Adam!" and "Will you play with us again tomorrow, Adam?" He nodded and gave high-fives all around. He was breathing heavy with the exertion of rolling the ball on the ground about 6,000 times. He went into the house, removing his T-shirt on the way to the kitchen, where he found Molly washing dishes.

The same dishes that he'd put into the dishwasher last night after her abrupt bedtime.

Adam just couldn't believe it. He happened to be a damn fun guy, and proving it was starting to get exhausting. Molly *had* to be deliberately refusing to enjoy his company, especially if she were resorting to doing a chore that had technically been done already.

Adam was almost looking forward to going back

to work on Monday, which had to be far less exerting than today had been. He'd never been so calculated about having a good time. Judging by his fatigue, it had almost crossed the line into work.

Well, he couldn't keep this up. Maybe it was time to throw in the towel.

Molly picked up *her* towel and dried the last dish, swirling around and around the dish until it squeaked. She rose on her toes and reached up to replace the dish on top of a stack in a cupboard, and when she flattened her feet back down, she sighed. Not an emotional sigh, not a lost-in-thought sigh. A tired sigh.

Adam peered a little more closely at Molly. Her unruly curls were pulled off her forehead with a thin headband, and dots of perspiration had popped up along her hairline.

She was tired. She was overdoing it. And he had a feeling that if he suggested that she was overdoing it, she would go out and mow her lawn *and* the lawn of her next-door neighbor just to prove she wasn't. She was the one who couldn't keep this up. She was going to wind up in the emergency room.

Flashing red lights speeding up his street. The deafening siren, getting even louder. Phone still in his hand...

No. He wasn't going to let that happen again to another person. He wasn't going to watch another person make it happen....

"Are you all right?"

Adam loosened his grip on his damp T-shirt, crumpled in his fist. “I’m fine. Are you all right?”

“I’m fine.”

Well, you will be, he thought. *As soon as I figure out how you’ll let me help you.*

Chapter Seven

"I have an idea."

Molly never met someone who was more full of ideas he wanted to share than Adam. That, of course, was not a bad character trait in itself, but when you were trying to avoid your former friend, who was now the man you married and kissed and lived with in the same house, this particular habit made it that much more difficult.

Molly tried to scrub the inside of the toilet harder and faster, the bright blue cleanser streaking down the curved sides, but she realized she'd been doing everything at maximum speed this weekend and there was really no way to further accelerate. But

Adam kept standing in the doorway waiting for a reaction or a response, so Molly said, "Oh?"

"And I promise, it doesn't involve any fun whatsoever. Nope, absolutely no fun. It's a chore, through and through. A big old chore."

Molly's ears perked up, but she didn't slow her pace. "Oh?"

"It's a chore that I noticed hasn't been done around here, and desperately needs doing."

Molly dropped the brush then and faced him. "That's not possible. I—" I did everything imaginable, and I'm starting to repeat myself, she thought Which even I know is silly and useless.

"Yes," Adam said, "and to be honest, it's starting to worry me."

"I did already call a few places for roof estimates, if that's what you mean," Molly said. "But there's no rain in the forecast this week." And the prices the roofers quoted, one after another, almost made me go into early labor, she silently added. She was going to try to put it off until she knew the results of her interview. Which was another reason she'd been going at top speed around here. She couldn't stand to dwell on the very real possibility of not getting that job. She'd done everything she could and, she thought, examining her husband's face, she was willing to bet it was far more than any of the other applicants.

"Well, that's good, but I'm not referring to that. It's time for some shopping. Let's go."

"What? Where?"

"The baby superstore."

Molly froze.

"Janine said there's a Baby World nearby," Adam said. "So I'm going to drive us over there. Your baby's not going to be able to sleep where he—or she—is right now for much longer. And although I'm perfectly willing to share the sofa bed, a crib might be more appropriate. And some other things. A whole lot of other things."

Her mind resisted, swirling and twisting her thoughts into incomprehension. Her skin broke out in a thin sweat, and she shivered. She tried to force herself to calm down. "I— But I have a lot to do today here."

"No, you don't. I saw you clean this bathroom yesterday. A professional maid only works eight hours a day. You're done. And this is something I'm sure you agree is much more important, right?"

"Right…"

"Right. And you might as well do this work now while you still have some energy. You might not feel up to it in a few weeks."

"I'll feel totally fine."

"*And* you might want to take advantage of the fact that I'm offering to help. You'll need a big brawny man to carry your heavy items."

"Oh, and what are you going to do, call him for me?"

"Good one, Jackson. Now, get in the damn car. Why are we standing around being unproductive?"

Molly searched for the slightest hint of amusement on Adam's face, which she half intended to smack right off. Because in using her own natural vocabulary, he sounded an awful lot as if he were making fun of her. But he seemed as serious as he could be, and it earned him a little of her respect.

However, it was not enough respect to allow him to be the one issuing orders. She struggled with the feeling trying to make its way to the surface, the way it had more and more in the past six months. She could fight it off again. It wasn't— It wasn't something she couldn't control.

"I'm driving," she said.

"Why?"

"Because," she said, willing her voice not to shake and betray her. "I know a way bigger store than Baby World. It's out on the other side of Rosewood."

"Let me guess. Baby Universe. Or Baby Galaxy?"

"And," she interrupted, "my car is bigger."

"Good point," he said. "Lead the way."

Molly pulled into the lot of Maybe Baby and swallowed hard. She watched women—bulging women, happy, glowing, excited women—heading toward the store, pushing carts. Some had men with their arms around their shoulders. Some had small children sitting in their carts, kicking their legs, singing nonsense or heartbreakingly screaming. Amazingly, the mothers of the screaming children seemed just as blithe and relaxed as the ones with quiet children.

Molly saw other women exiting the store, pushing carts spilling over with colorful boxes, and their kids were dancing along the concrete, clutching balloons and their mothers' hands, or crying at a balloon let loose in a zigzagging ascent, out of reach forever.

Molly swallowed again. She'd been lucky in her first three months to not have much difficulty with morning sickness, but maybe parking-lot sickness was a lesser known pregnancy side effect. She'd have to check on the Internet later.

"I know what you're thinking," Adam said.

Molly turned to him, guilt heating her cheeks.

"You want a balloon," Adam said. "A grown, serious woman like yourself? You ought to be ashamed. Well, okay, I'll get you one today, but we'll have to do something about this in the future."

"Shut up," Molly said mildly, relieved he hadn't been able to read her mind. He *would* have been ashamed of her, at least as ashamed as she was of herself.

She got out of the car, locked it behind them and walked toward the entrance with purposeful strides. But she slowed as she became part of the small crowd of customers, moving around her, going in and out. Why did she feel so out of place, out of step? If they were not here— If they were all in an office, for example, Molly just knew she could run confident rings around all these strangers. How come here, now, she felt like a lost little girl? How could all these women around her have everything under happy control while she, *she,* was suddenly paralyzed with helplessness?

Adam, who she hadn't even noticed had left her side, wheeled a bright red shopping cart over to where she now stood still. "Okay, Mom," he said. "Let's get started."

She forced her feet to move, and the two sliding doors slid apart as magically as if she'd said, "Open sesame." And there she and Adam stood, facing an airplane-hangar-size interior filled—filled—with shelves and rows and aisles of *things.*

A bloodcurdling shriek went off in Molly's ear, nearly confirming she'd stepped into a horror movie, but it was just an infant in his mother's arms, angry at something. His mother was as serene as the Virgin Mary.

"Excuse me," Molly heard behind her, and realized they were still hovering in front of the entrance. She peripherally saw Adam there next to her, probably just as clueless.

"Where do I start?" Molly mumbled, her gaze running from ceiling to floor, her bottom lip starting to shake. "I don't know where to start."

Adam moved before she could, pushing the cart

down the first aisle they came to, which was actually in the middle of about forty aisles in total.

Strollers.

Molly had never seen anything like it. When she had bought her car last year, she had walked into the dealership with folders of her detailed research, sure that she knew as much or more than the salesman himself, and wheeled and dealed herself into the car she wanted at the price she could afford. The dealership supervisor also offered her a job before she left in her new car.

But here, where this all should have been on a similar but more manageable, baby-size scale, it was incomprehensible. Stroller after stroller, big ones, little ones, ones for multiple babies, all with different features.

A saleswoman demonstrated one oversize, complicated stroller for two pregnant women who appeared to be twin sisters.

"The Walkaround 5000 is *the* top-of-the-line stroller product," the saleswoman said, smiling. She showed the different angles the baby could be maneuvered into, from prone to sitting up to inversion. "It's very popular with celebrities. You've probably seen in it magazines." The twin women nodded, staring entranced.

Adam eyed the sticker price. "Nine hundred dollars?" he asked. "What else can you do with that thing, strap your kid in and launch him to Jupiter for the day?"

The three women smiled at him, unoffended, unaffected. Everyone was smiling, Molly realized, like they were all in a loud, spinning funhouse.

She hurried away and rounded the corner. She put her forearm on a shelf to steady herself, and cried out in alarm when a stuffed bear asked her, with a moving mouth, "Hello, what's your name?" She backed into the shelf across from it, knocking over a box that began playing "Old MacDonald" as soon as it hit the floor. She ran now, turned another corner and found herself surrounded with sheets and blankets, all in soft, soothing pastel hues that made her dizzy.

"Hi," she heard, and she whirled to find a woman about her age, and about her current size. "Are you okay?"

Molly nodded.

"When are you due?" the woman asked, and smiled that contented smile.

"I—I don't know," Molly whispered.

"Molly?" she heard in the distance.

"Why can't I do this?" she demanded of the woman, who retreated a step, her smile wobbling a bit with puzzlement.

Adam jogged up the aisle. He'd abandoned their empty cart. "Molly?"

"It's getting small in here," Molly said. "The walls—they're closing. I can't breathe."

She leaned into Adam and he held her, and suddenly there were two saleswomen there, too, and a cup of water was pressed into her hand. "Let's take her into the family room so she can sit a minute," one said. "Does she have panic attacks often?"

"I don't think so," Adam said.

"I'm fine," Molly mumbled, clinging to Adam.

The women opened a side door to reveal a small, bright yellow room, with a few breastfeeding women and several kids running back and forth. Molly shook her head and planted her feet.

"Thank you so much," Adam said, "but I have a feeling my wife needs some air more than anything."

He led Molly back through the carnival dreamland of a store. "It's okay, we're almost outside," he told her over and over. She allowed him to maneuver her gently into a bench outside near the entrance.

She sat and took in a deep breath of fresh air. Then she took a sip of water, and continued that way for a few minutes. Breathe, sip, breathe, sip.

Adam's worried eyes were watching her face, very close. "I think we need to take you to the doctor."

"It's Sunday."

"The hospital, then."

She waited a few minutes. She felt back to normal. The baby kicked a good healthy, annoyed kick. "I'm fine, physically," she said. "I don't need the hospital."

"I'm not arguing about this," Adam said. "Call your doctor."

She pulled out her cell, speed dialed the ob/gyn, had him paged, and then had a five-minute question-

and-answer with the doctor while Adam paced in front of the bench. When she hung up, she had a just-in-case appointment for the following morning.

She sipped her last sip and crumpled the cup.

"Are you sure, completely sure, you don't want to see the doctor now?" Adam said.

"Yes. He asked me plenty I told him everything."

"Thank you for doing that."

"Don't thank me. I had to. I don't want to jeopardize the baby. But I really do think I'm fine. It's—" She didn't want to say what she was thinking, but she didn't want to go to the hospital, either, so she said, "It's just a mental meltdown."

She watched people go in and out, but she was removed just enough from them to do it passively, and not with the panic building again.

"What happened in there?" Adam asked, sitting down beside her.

Molly couldn't look at him. "I had to get out of there. I—I don't know why I can't do this."

"Do what?"

"It seems like too much. And it shouldn't, right? Because I know how to handle too much. I *know* how."

Adam didn't answer her. He'd had a nagging feeling that's what this was all about, and why the nursery had stayed empty. "Tell me," he urged. "Tell me."

"I love that I'm having a baby. I love my baby."

"I know. Anyone could tell."

She seemed momentarily placated by that, but

then her face darkened again. "I'm—I'm—I'm *scared,* okay?" she said quietly. "This whole time, I've been trying not to say that out loud. But I am. I'm so freaking scared. I'm supposed to be able to do it all, have it all, aren't I? The modern career mom? But I don't know anything about the 'mom' part. And I don't really have anyone to ask. I don't want to ask my own mother, or she'll think I'm in over my head. All I know is from independent research. And I surf on the Internet and I read *Consumer Reports* and I can't make sense of any of it. What do I need? Everything? How can I afford everything in there? How do I know what's better than something else?

"I'm so used to trying for the best," Molly went on, "but I can't figure any of this out. Now my baby won't get the best because I have no idea where to even start. That nursery in my house is like a ghost town because I'm scared to go in there. I'm *scared* to go in there and mess everything up. I'm scared, and I *hate* that word. This is too much for me. It's too damn much for me."

She put her head in her hands, and Adam thought fast. "Okay, Molly," he began, "what if, say, a client came up to you and said, 'Ms. Jackson, I just don't know what to do. We have this massive project that we haven't even started. We're a complete mess. We're really in a bind.' What would you say?"

"But it's not that easy…"

"That's what the client is insisting. 'It's too difficult, Ms. Jackson. We're screwed. We're all screwed.' But you, Ms. Jackson, know they're not screwed because you've seen plenty of companies in their same situation who've successfully completed similar projects. So what would you say?"

Molly shook her head.

"Come on, Molly. You're a professional. This person's counting on your advice. What would you say?"

She sighed. "I'd say, 'What's your time frame?'"

"Three months."

"Three months. Well, okay, three months is doable for anything." Then Molly stopped, as if surprised at what she heard come out of her own mouth.

"You're kidding," Adam said. "'Three months? No way, we're screwed. We don't even know where to start."

"Well," she said slowly, "first you have to make yourself see the project is not so unmanageable. Break it down into individual tasks with individual deadlines, and then do some delegating."

"How do we do that?" Adam asked. "Are you suggesting, dare I say it, that we make—a *list?*"

He saw a burning spark ignite in Molly's eyes. A different man, a man who wasn't Molly's best friend, would possibly interpret that heat a different way—because it looked a lot like attraction, desire for him, desire to lean over and take his face in her hands and kiss him deeply, probe his mouth with her tongue and—

Right. But he was in a position to *not* misinterpret that spark. It was, he knew, the idea of organization that turned her on.

Molly nodded.

"That's just what I thought," he said. "Wait here."

He got up and sprinted back into Maybe Baby. He scanned the signs suspended from the ceiling and ran over to customer service.

"Yes?" the woman said, smiling. This place certainly was friendly. Almost made you wonder.

"Suppose a woman was to, I guess, register for presents, like—"

"Like for a baby shower?"

"Yes, exactly. Do you have like a big master list of things to pick out?"

The woman appeared delighted to hand over a thick stapled stack of paper, and it was likely because registered moms brought in truckloads of business.

"Thanks," he said, and ran.

"You can also use the Maybe Baby Web site!" he heard the woman call after him. The sliding doors parted and he landed on the bench next to Molly. He held up the papers.

"Holy crap," Molly said.

"Ms. Jackson, that's hardly what a professional like you would say to a desperate client. Now, I have here some raw data. Can we make some sense of this?"

Molly put a hand on her purse.

"Yup," Adam said. "That's what I'm talking about.

Grab a pen and some paper and we're off and running. You're going to make a schedule, and a budget, and you're going to delegate some things to my mom, and Janine, and me."

Molly withdrew a pen from her purse and uncapped it with her teeth while she pulled out a pad of paper. Then she glanced at him, a little uncertainly, the blue plastic cap still in her mouth.

He reached over and took hold of the cap. She separated her front teeth, and he removed it, slipping it into his pocket. "You can do this," he said. "I have faith in you, remember?"

They sat on the bench and worked for a long time. Molly was incredible. She drew up a miniature spreadsheet in some kind of shorthand. She scheduled shopping for particular items only on specific days, and budgeted spending only a certain amount per week. She assigned tasks to others to do, like comparing prices of big-ticket items online and assembling the furniture when they got it home. She even picked lavender for the baby's room, and let Adam choose the other color. He went with yellow, the brightest, cheeriest color there was.

When Molly lifted her head from the papers in her lap, they had been sitting there two hours past their expected lunchtime. Adam had seen a few salespeople sneak out for ten-minute breaks, appearing surprised to see Adam and Molly still taking up the bench space, still working. Adam stood, stretched his arms over his head, and took Molly's arm, leading her to her car.

In the driver's seat once again, Molly shuffled through her papers of hard work, stacked them neatly and looked up at Adam. There was that spark again. That spark in her eyes that Adam was not going to misinterpret or mistake for anything but excitement for the completed task at hand, as—

As Molly's lips on his, as Molly's hands on his cheeks, tangling her fingers into his hair and grasping, her tongue pushing into his mouth. Adam couldn't gasp if he wanted to, because Molly was there, for real, and it wasn't physically possible.

He reached around and clasped the back of her head, his hand caressing the warm skin of her neck. Molly moaned into him and he tried to turn his right shoulder in, to press the whole top half of his body against hers, but he couldn't because…there, the seat belt was. He fumbled with the catch, popped it open and now he could wrap both arms around her shoulders, hold her closer.

Molly beat him to it—her hands had already moved down his back and came around his waist. She tugged the hem of his T-shirt out of his jeans, slipping her hands inside, and this time he did pull away from her to gasp in an openmouthed breath as her fingernails dug in to the sensitive skin there.

She pushed her mouth onto his again, and clawed at his top button. He reached back to try to recline her seat, but this wasn't his car and his hand found only unfamiliar air.

He broke their heated kiss to turn his head down to glance at the seat, but before he could do it, Molly wasn't on him anymore, she wasn't— She was sitting back in her own seat, gripping the steering wheel so hard her wrists were shaking. A mother was hurrying her oblivious toddler away from Molly's car, looking over her shoulder once at the R-rated scene she was trying to shield her child from. Adam was relieved to see the curious half smile on her face, so he knew she wasn't running for a security guard, but he—Molly and he—

They didn't risk looking at one another. They didn't say a word. They both breathed hard from the exertion of wanting and almost having. Molly started the car, put it into Reverse, then Drive, and carefully steered them out of the parking lot.

When they got back home, she parked in the driveway, just as carefully and deliberately as if Adam were a stranger administering her first road test. Then she opened the door, lurched out of her seat and slammed the door so quickly that Adam didn't feel right getting out with her. This was her way of exiting, and he was going to let her do it the way she had to.

And that way was to hurry up the walk, unlock the door and disappear into the house.

Chapter Eight

Rebecca loitered at the end of Sylvia's walkway, chatting animatedly to their elderly neighbor, when Molly arrived home. Both women waved at her as she pulled in the drive, but they must have expected her to go in to her house, because as she approached them, they abruptly quit in the middle of their conversation and turned two innocent smiles on her.

"You were talking about me," Molly accused, out of breath from just walking about twenty feet. Depressing.

"Please. You're imagining things," Rebecca said. "Where were you? Thought you'd be inside working."

"I had an ob/gyn appointment."

The smiles morphed into looks of concern. "Everything's all right?" Sylvia asked.

"Yes," Molly assured them. "I didn't feel too well in Maybe Baby yesterday, and I just thought I'd check in."

"That place would make anyone not feel well," Rebecca said. "I once stopped in there to buy a baby gift for a friend, and it was complete pandemonium. I waited on line to pay for almost an hour."

Molly felt grateful, and a tiny bit vindicated. "It certainly is a bit—overwhelming."

"More than a bit," Sylvia said. "But I'll let you in on a little secret, Molly—and Rebecca, you keep this in mind for the future. In my day, we didn't have any of the stuff they sell in that store. And guess what? Everybody lived."

Rebecca laughed, and Molly squeezed Sylvia's hand. "I'll remember that."

"You ought to."

Molly wondered if the older woman would have some kind of sage advice on how to forget about that kiss yesterday. She hadn't even known why she'd all but jumped Adam, couldn't remember the immediate moments preceding it. She had been just so relieved, so happy, so full of confidence again, and Adam was there, and her brain, maybe tired from overuse, had checked out and let her body take over. Her body had felt it all night, felt it in the dark air that Adam breathed also in another part of the house, where she could've just gone to him, and—

She shook her head. But she could shake her head until it fell off, and she wouldn't shake off the memory of the most amazing feeling she'd ever had. With *Adam...*

"What is it, dear?" Sylvia asked.

"Maybe we need a subject change," Rebecca said, patting Molly on the arm. "I have a question anyway, and I feel I can trust both of you to be discreet. What do you know about Jack Lever?"

"Jack Lever up the street?" Molly asked, trying to get her mind on her friend. "He's a lawyer, a widower. Two kids..."

"Or do you mean, is he seeing anybody?" Sylvia asked with a wink.

"Well," Rebecca began, but then saw something over Molly's shoulder that made her frown. "Oh, never mind, we'll talk about it another time. Here comes trouble. Rhonda Johnson and Irene Dare-to-be-a-huge-pain-in-the—"

"Hush, dear," Sylvia said, but not without an appreciative smile.

"Hi, ladies," Irene greeted them. It was amazing how without having even turned around, Molly could hear that woman's sneer.

"Molly," Rhonda said, "we stopped by hoping to catch a glimpse of your new fiancé."

Molly straightened her spine the best she could

with all her extra weight up front. It was time to face the inevitable Danbury Way music, but after surviving her wedding and her interview and her Maybe Baby meltdown and that first unbelievable, unforgettable kiss and that second frighteningly hot make-out, this was nothing. This could actually be enjoyable. "Watch this," she silently mouthed to Sylvia and Rebecca, then whirled on Mutt and Jeff.

"I'm sorry to disappoint you," Molly said, her voice even. "But I no longer have a fiancé."

Someone gasped, and Molly was sure she saw Irene lick her lips in anticipation of the most delicious kind of gossip. "Oh, Molly," she said, "how sad for you. I'm so sorry to hear that."

"What happened?" Rhonda cut in, foregoing any pretense of sympathy in order to get right to the good stuff.

"Well, what happened is, I got married," Molly said. "So, I no longer have a fiancé. Because I have a husband."

Four mouths hung open. Sylvia was the first to speak. "Oh, the way that boy looked at you, I just knew he couldn't wait long."

"What way he looked at me?" Molly asked, but Rebecca had already snatched up her left hand and held it an inch from her face.

"You're married!" she cried. "Molly, congratulations!"

Irene and Rhonda glared at each other, perhaps

each mentally accusing the other of missing the story of the century. "Hold on a minute," Irene said. "You got engaged *and* married in the space of a week?"

"Six days," Molly corrected.

"Isn't that a little..." Rhonda began.

"What?" Molly demanded.

"I was going to say, unusual?" Rhonda said.

Molly tried not to let her face give her secrets away. Rhonda couldn't know anything. She was just hoping something about the fast marriage was fishy, and was looking to trip Molly up. She couldn't know anything, Molly mentally reassured herself.

"I think a whirlwind romance is lovely, something every woman dreams about," Sylvia admonished in her gentle way. "And you *should* meet Adam. I never saw a man who adored someone more. Why, Rhonda," she continued, as sweet as coconut cream pie, "I never noticed before—I always thought your eyes were brown. But they're such a beautiful shade of...green."

"What are you implying?" Rhonda bit out. "That I'm *jealous?*"

"I didn't say that at all," Sylvia said, appearing shocked. "Did I?"

Rhonda stomped away.

"You are my new role model," Molly heard Rebecca whisper to Sylvia.

Irene appeared torn between running after her friend and staying to collect more dirt, but a sound from inside the house froze her in her tracks.

Howling.

Molly smiled. Elmer, like his owner, had a keen sense of timing.

"Listen, you and Rhonda might not want to bring your dogs around here too often anymore," Molly said to Irene. "I have a dog now, too, and he's not very friendly to dogs who are, well, smaller and weaker."

Irene scurried down the block.

Molly held back a giggle at having portrayed little floppy Elmer as a huge attack dog.

"Your happy news is going to be all over town in approximately eight minutes," Rebecca said.

"Fine," Molly said. "Let them spread a true story, for a change." *Let someone else do our dirty work for us,* she heard Adam say in her memory, and she was proud she hadn't backed down. "Meanwhile," she said, "I have a ton of work to do."

"I love how you always say that like it's not something you dread," Rebecca said.

"It's not," Molly said. "See you two later."

"'Bye," they chimed together, and Molly walked up to her own door, but she could swear she heard them whisper a few words behind her. *I'm seriously paranoid,* she thought. *They're my friends.*

She jiggled her key in the lock and her phone began to ring.

"I'm coming, I'm coming," Molly called, although she knew that never worked. She shoved on her front door and hurried to the phone. "Shh," she hushed Elmer, now barking at the phone. "Hello?" she answered, trying not to pant.

As she listened to the voice on the other end congratulate her and deliver the news she'd been waiting for, her grin widened and widened.

The job was hers.

She'd avoided her worst-case scenario. Crisis averted.

It wasn't until she hung up the phone and spied a rumpled sheet corner peeking out from under one sofa cushion that she realized something. Her worst-case scenario had no longer been the fear of becoming destitute and hard up for money.

It had been the thought of Adam, no longer needed for her cover story, packing his suitcase and leaving.

"How's married life treating you?" Janine asked around a mouthful of chef's salad.

Adam set down his cup of lemonade. "What kind of question is that?"

"The kind of question married people get asked," Janine pointed out, waving her fork at him. A little drop of Italian dressing landed under his eye. "And anyway, what kind of *answer* is that?"

"I don't know," he said, rubbing his finger under his eye. "Forget it."

Janine shrugged. "Okay. Hey, thanks for lunch."

Adam glanced around the crowded café that was about equidistant from his job at Gibraltar Foods and his sister's job. He'd finally called her for a lunch date after he'd been completely unable to focus at work for the last three hours. Of course, that normally wouldn't be such a big deal to him, except that he wanted to focus on anything but how he was going to react to Molly when he ran into her again.

They'd eased around each other last night, not meeting each others' eyes, and he'd left this morning before she'd come downstairs, but there was no avoiding his wife this evening.

"So—" he started, then stopped, feeling not unlike a big idiot.

"What?" Janine broke a roll in half, then peered up at Adam again. She dropped both bread pieces on her plate. "What's wrong?" she asked, searching his face.

"Well," he began awkwardly, "you're a woman."

"And you're a genius," she replied, wide-eyed. "Gosh, I never *could* figure out why I needed a bra and tampons. Thanks for solving the ongoing mystery."

"Let me finish, will you?" Adam asked. "I mean, you're a woman who's been pregnant twice. I have a question about all those hormones everyone talks about. Is it true?"

"Is what true, exactly?"

"About the hormones."

"Adam," Janine said, "if you need me to explain a particular fact of the birds and the bees to you, you need to be a little more specific with what you're looking for."

"Listen, I happen to be a field expert on both the birds and the bees. On that subject, I'm more of a naturalist than Audubon."

"Your ladies' man reputation always did precede you."

He was going nowhere. "Okay, fine. I'll ask you the question, but you can't ask why I'm asking."

She spread butter on her bread. "Out with it, already."

He cleared his throat. "Would all those pregnancy hormones, say, make a woman suddenly, out of nowhere, jump a guy?"

The bread stopped halfway to Janine's mouth, and she dropped it on her plate again. "You saw Molly jump a guy?"

"I never said Molly. This is purely, one hundred percent hypothetical. Let me try again. Would hormones make a nameless pretend woman—with absolutely *no* warning, I might add—jump her nameless pretend husband? And then, also with zero warning, stop in the middle of things and refuse to talk about it, say, for the rest of the night and next morning?"

He had to hand it to his sister. She just sat there calmly chewing on a cucumber slice as though she really were pondering complex theoretical implications and not her younger brother's actual love life. Then she gulped down some ice water and said, "Here's the thing. When I was pregnant, I jumped on every man I met."

"No, you didn't."

"I did. Attacked and made out with every one of them. The mailman. The guy at the movie rental place. The dry cleaner. A toll taker on the New York Thruway."

"This testimony is ringing false, somehow."

"So, my advice to you is," Janine said, "if Molly kisses you again, don't overthink it. Don't worry about what comes next. You need to just go ahead and let her do what she wants. Let her jump you. Let her rip your clothes off and have her way with you in the middle of the living room floor."

"I can't do that," Adam lied.

"Yes, you can," Janine said, her nod solemn. "You can do it. Do it for the baby."

"You're out of your mind," he said, "if you think I'm buying this. I see your evil motive. You *like* Molly and you want us to stay married so she can be a permanent card-carrying member of the Shibbs Girls' club."

She gave him a pitying look. "If you weren't going to trust my opinion, then why'd you ask me at all?"

"That's what I'm wondering myself."

"Well, stop wondering because *I* know why," Janine said. "You asked me because you knew I would tell you to go for it and that's exactly what you want. You just want someone to tell you it's okay. It's more than okay. Be her husband for real. Clearly that's what she wants."

"You don't know what you're talking about. She wants me about as much as I want her."

Janine snorted. "That's probably true enough."

The waiter dropped the check and Adam ducked his sister's lingering smirk by pulling out his wallet. As he counted out a few bills, Janine said, "Just call Mom and ask her instead if you won't take advice from me."

"I'm not going to discuss this topic with our mother."

"Why not? Do the hypothetical question thing. Very effective. I'm sure she'll have no idea you're referring to Molly. And she'll totally agree with me. I guarantee it." She stuck out her tongue and suddenly stood. "Thanks again for lunch. I, um, I'm late."

She almost tipped over her chair in her rush to exit the café. Adam raised his eyebrows and watched his sister through the front window. She jogged across the street, looked back at the restaurant once, and began frantically pawing through her oversize leather handbag.

Aha. That sneak. Going for the cell phone. Trying to get to their mother first, was she? Two could play at that juvenile game. Adam slipped his own phone out of his pocket and hit one button. He put the phone to his ear just as Janine flipped open her phone and started pressing a series of buttons.

Moments like these were why he had his mother's house on speed dial. He would not let his sister get to Mom first and tell her everything and then have her call Adam. If his mother was going to bother to give him advice on this, he needed it to be purely objective, uncolored by his sister's good intentions.

"Hello?" his mother answered.

Adam glanced out the window again and saw Janine stomp her foot on the sidewalk in reaction to the busy signal. She cast a dark, dangerous scowl at the café before getting into her car and driving off. "Hey, Mom."

"Hi, love."

"Would a pregnant woman's hormones make her kiss a man she ordinarily wouldn't kiss if she was in her regular right mind?" Might as well cut right to the chase. This was embarrassing enough.

A few beats of silence went by. He hoped she didn't pass out or anything. "Mom?"

"I'm here," she said, and her voice was like a warm familiar pillow. "Let me think. It's been a while. And, you know, hormones do very different things to different women. I'm sure a doctor couldn't even tell you for sure."

"But, what do you think?"

"I think," she said carefully, "as someone not in the medical field, that out-of-whack hormones could very well make a person act in a way counter to her normal behavior."

Adam didn't expect the sharp pang of disappointment, but said nothing.

"However," Pam went on, "if that person's normal behavior is to mask her true feelings, then acting counter to her normal behavior would be to let her true feelings come out. And so she'd be acting *more* honest and, ironically, *more* like herself."

"Um. Right. So how do I, er, how does someone tell for sure?"

"I just don't know. Depends on the person, on the situation and on the hormones, I suppose."

Adam raked a hand through his hair and looked around the café to make sure no one was listening to his half of the bizarre conversation. "Okay, well, thanks."

"A friend of yours having woman trouble?"

Adam smiled at his mother's soft subtlety, a contrast to Janine's bluntness. "A friend of mine, right."

"I'm afraid I'm not very much help to him. Sounds like he's just as confused as the woman he's involved with. Like maybe he didn't quite expect what he got himself into?"

Adam closed his eyes for a second. "Yeah."

"Maybe he just needs to be there for her in all the ways he can."

"She doesn't let anyone in."

"Why should she have to? He already has a key. All he's got to do is use it, and let himself in."

Adam sat for a moment, among the eating, chatting customers in the café, and absorbed his mother's metaphor.

"Thanks, Mom."

"No problem. Next time you call, we can talk

about you and Molly instead. I'd like to know how you're both doing."

He heard the smile in her request.

"I'll keep you updated," he said. "I promise."

Adam stood outside the front door with his key in his hand. Molly had had it made for him last week. He turned it over and over now, examining every groove. It caught a glare from the sun over his shoulder, but he supposed that after a year of coming and going, the key would dull and darken. When it lost its luster, he still wasn't going to want to give it up, even though that was part of the deal.

Plans changed. Maybe that plan would also. Maybe he could have a hand in it.

He inserted the key into the lock and pushed the door open at the same time Molly pulled the knob on the other side. She stumbled back, and Adam stumbled forward, and both reached out to steady themselves on the door frame. Which was how they ended up in a tangle of arms, their faces inches apart.

The memory of their searing hot kiss was too recent not to be tempted by it when they were this close. Molly's gaze bounced to his lips, then his eyes, then back to his mouth. Adam felt blood pounding through his chest, in his ears and pushing hard below his belt.

"I have to tell you something," Molly said.

Adam was taken aback. He had been so sure that he would be the first to say whatever it was she was about to say. He didn't think she'd admit it before he did, admit what was sizzling there in the air....

"I got the job," she said.

Adam blinked, and retreated a step. "You—you got the job," he repeated. He moved away from the door, farther from the bare, lily-scented skin of her arms.

She licked her lips and also took a step back. "Yes."

"Good," he said, then realized it wasn't enough. "Fantastic. Amazing. Great," he reiterated, hoping the superlative words were enough without the inflection behind them. He couldn't muster it right this second, just when he was reminded this was all a setup with a purpose.

"What did the doctor say?" he asked.

"Just stress."

"Just stress, eh?" he replied. "Imagine that. And you're going to cut down on that stress, right?"

"Sure." She watched his face, but he didn't know what she saw there that made her add, "About yesterday—"

"No," he interrupted, and she tucked in her chin, withdrawing in apparent surprise. "You don't have to explain, or—talk about it, or—I understand."

"You do?"

"Yesterday was yesterday, and today is today. It's all right," he said, releasing her from whatever obligation had driven her to finally address the issue. He didn't want to hear her say she was embarrassed. He also didn't want to hear her say it wouldn't happen again.

He didn't want to hear her tell him that he was only an item on her list, due to be crossed out this time next year.

Why I Might Have Been Too Hasty in Saying I Couldn't Live with Adam Shibbs for a Year:

1. Not only is Adam friendly with every single type of person in existence, but for some reason, they're all willing to share their expertise with him.

Like Tuesday evening, Molly thought, when he brought two burly guys over here, bought them three large pizzas and then the trio clomped upstairs and proceeded to fix the roof.

Adam never said he was going to do that.

Molly went back to her list.

2. He made the nursery a—a nursery.

Again foregoing casual mention, Adam spent Wednesday afternoon assembling a crib and hammering in some shelves into the wall of the formerly empty room. He added a beanbag bear and monkey, who smiled at Molly every time she peeked in there. And she did peek in there sometimes, now that the door stayed open.

Suddenly the room was breathing life, and as crazy

as Molly would have considered it if anyone had asked her only weeks ago, it was because of Adam.

3. Adam brought me a pillow when I was working earlier.

Molly felt for the soft pillow now and readjusted it at the small of her back. She'd thanked Adam in surprise when he'd brought it, but he didn't reply. His sort-of-grunt was the only indication he'd heard her.

Elmer stirred under Molly's chair, and laid his warm head on her feet. She reached down to scratch behind his ears.

Adam had morphed into the ideal roommate, which should have thrilled her.

Instead, she kept thinking that he wasn't her roommate. He was her husband. And she tried *not* to think about how much she was starting to want a real one. *This* real one.

Chapter Nine

"Let's go out," Adam said.

Molly looked up from the newspaper business section. Was she imagining it, or did Adam sound like his old self again? This entire week, he'd been—well, certainly not ignoring her. He'd been going out of his way to attend to her every anticipated need. But his cheerfulness, his come-play-with-me attitude had disappeared, and though she had all but told him to take it away from her in the first place, she hadn't expected him to ever actually do it, and she *really* hadn't expected to actually miss it.

So this sudden turnaround surprised her, and pleased her, and therefore annoyed her. "I'm busy," she murmured, trying to sound firm but not having the heart to sound harsh. She buried her face in the stocks page again.

"It's Friday night," he persisted.

She looked up. "Why are you suddenly…"

"What?"

"I don't know. Sounding like yourself."

"You're weird."

"No, *you're* weird," she countered.

"Great comeback. Throw some shoes on and let's go for a walk. It's a beautiful night, might as well enjoy it. It'll be winter soon."

"Oh, right. Three months from now."

He turned up the wattage on the Shibbs smile. "Come on." She was about to give in, to grab her flip-flops by the door and walk outside, when she caught his glance out the window at—at Rebecca's house?

Her mind clicked back to spotting him deep in conversation with Rebecca on the sidewalk the other day. She ignored the rising jealousy and turned her memory back again, to Rebecca and Sylvia whispering when Molly walked away. *"Aha,"* Molly said. "I'm on to you. I've smoked this whole conspiracy out."

"What?" Adam asked, and the wide-eyed innocent expression on his face confirmed it.

"I can't believe they got you in on it. You're supposed to be committed to being sneaky with me, and now you're sneaky with them. You're a Danbury Way double agent."

"I have no idea what 'them' you are referring to, my darling wife."

"It's a baby shower," she said. "There's a baby shower tonight for me. At Rebecca's. And you're supposed to get me there. Right?"

Adam opened his mouth an inch and turned his head to begin to shake it.

"Don't deny it," Molly warned.

Adam said nothing.

"Damn," she said, grinding her back teeth together. "I hoped this wouldn't happen. I don't want to be the center of attention. It's difficult enough what we're doing. Everyone in one place, asking me questions about us, about the baby..."

"I can't believe you," Adam said, his smile fading. "Your friends are doing a nice, generous thing for you, and you just have to resist. You can't let it happen. Because you didn't plan it."

"That's not it at all."

"You said at Maybe Baby that you had no one to talk to," Adam pointed out. "There will be a whole room of women, many of whom have had babies, who all are there just for the reason of celebrating *your* baby. They'll help if you ask them. They're your friends."

"But—"

"I know from firsthand experience that you're a good friend. You're always there when anyone needs you. The other part of being a good friend is letting people be there for you when you need them. It's reciprocal."

Molly had a strong feeling he was talking about himself as much as the houseful of women two doors down waiting for her. "All right," she said, hoping he understood she included him in her concession. "Okay. Let me go change my clothes, at least."

"Good. And, uh, try not to look too nice," Adam said. "Or they'll know you know."

Molly rolled her eyes and went into her room. She pulled on a light blue maternity sundress that she'd been avoiding because it was so— It just screamed, "I'm pregnant!" But, she supposed, as guest of honor at her own shower, it was probably appropriate to be obvious. Besides, the baby was more and more *there* every day. She'd noticed strangers watching her in the grocery store or in the post office with a mixture of curiosity and care, as if it were a neighborhood's job to keep an eye on a pregnant woman. It made Molly feel like the circus fat lady, but what if what Adam had said was right? That people wanted to be there if you needed them.

It was a nice, comforting thought. She wondered if Adam always had those kinds of thoughts, and if that's why he was so much more relaxed. She made a mental note for the next time she had to reach a top shelf for the peanut butter at the supermarket—to look for someone taller and ask for assistance. Just as an experiment.

She twisted her tired, humidity-beaten hair into a thick braid, slipped on beige sandals and stepped back into the living room. "How's this? Too nice? Should I spill some grape juice down my front or something?"

Adam stared at her for a long time without answering. "You're perfect," he finally said. "There's no way you couldn't be."

Molly didn't have an answer, but a recent memory of his face flashed in front of her eyes—his jaw slack, his lips swollen, his eyes half-closed as she frantically yanked at his clothes in the car last weekend. She willed it away but, disturbingly, found the current Adam standing there, four feet from her, to be no less sexy.

"Let's go," she said. "Are you supposed to give Rebecca some kind of signal?"

"She's watching out her window for us," he admitted. "I'm supposed to lure you out for a walk. She also asked me to try to distract you somehow from seeing people arriving at her house before, but I had a little feeling that part wouldn't be difficult. You've been glued to the paper for the last forty-five minutes. You wouldn't have noticed if her house had gone up in flames."

Molly grinned at herself. "I'm focused."

"No kidding."

They left the house and Molly was careful not to look at Rebecca's property. They turned right and walked past Carly's, and as they neared the next house, Rebecca stuck her head out the window. "Oh, Molly!" she cried, as if surprised by her luck. "Is Adam with you? I need help! Something's wrong with the sink and it's flooding the kitchen! Help!"

Adam sprinted to Rebecca's door in an Academy Award–worthy performance. Molly rolled her eyes and ad-libbed her own lines. "Do you need me to call a plumber?"

"I already did!" Rebecca called back. Adam entered the house, and Molly followed a few steps behind.

Even knowing full well what was coming, the loud, collective, joyful shouts and squeals of "Surprise!" really did make her stumble back. If she hadn't been expecting it at all, she probably would have landed flat on her butt in the foyer.

For a full minute, all she could see was a crowd of faces and balloons and laughing. A few flashbulbs went off, documenting her face for years to come.

But one by one, her friends approached her, kissing her cheek, patting her belly, putting a flute of sparkling cider into her hand, and she was able to greet each of them with genuine appreciation.

There was Angela Schumacher from down the block and her little girl, Olivia, who, with a pink party hat crookedly perched on her head, appeared thrilled to be a part of the grown-ups' party. Molly hugged them both, and asked Olivia, "How did everyone keep this secret from me?" The seven-year-old shrugged, clearly amused.

Carly Alderson was there, too, as beautiful as ever, but lately, the glow in her cheeks was not from expensive makeup. She had recently fallen madly in love with local contractor Bo Conway, and her happiness radiated from every pore. "You should bottle that man and sell it in spas," Molly whispered in her ear. "You'd make a fortune."

"I'm sure, but I can't bring myself to share him," Carly whispered back, and winked.

"Can't say I blame you," Molly said, then stiffened slightly when she noticed Megan Schumacher, Angela's sister, hovering behind Carly. Love had transformed Megan herself recently, but as that love had bloomed with Carly's ex-husband, Greg, there had been some bad blood and trampled feelings. Molly was relieved when Carly turned, caught Megan's eye, and the two acknowledged one another with a small but civil nod.

Megan was the next one to hug Molly, and Molly made sure Carly had moved away before saying, "Thank you for coming. It must be so hard for both you and Carly to be here, but—"

"Please don't even think about it. This is your night, and we're here as your friends," Megan said, her pretty face earnest. "We're both fine. Really. We just want to celebrate you and your baby."

Molly, deeply touched at the mutual gesture of both

women, embraced Megan again and blew a kiss at Carly, who had turned around on the other side of the room. Carly lifted her glass and tilted it toward her.

Rebecca trotted over and grabbed Molly from behind. "Look, I can't reach my hands!" she cried, encircling Molly's waist as tight as she could with her arms and waving her fingers in front of her.

"Oh, get off me," Molly said, pushing her aside and laughing with the others. "Flooded sink, my behind."

"It was the best I could come up with," Rebecca confessed. "I can't believe Adam ran to the door like that. What a hero. For a second there, I thought he forgot I was making it up."

"Speaking of you, Adam, some of us haven't met you yet," Angela piped up.

"I have!" her daughter shouted, and Angela's eyes widened.

"Wait. *You're* the Adam my kids were going on about? Who played kickball with them last week?"

"Yes, ma'am," Adam said.

"I thought they were talking about a new *kid* they met." She chuckled at herself. "Well, you're popular already. So stand right there, Adam, and let the adults ogle you for a few minutes."

Adam turned on his heel, posing and hamming it up. The guests cheered. Molly felt herself turning red.

"I think I was officially the first to meet him," Marti Vincente called. "He proposed to Molly at Entrée, and I got a front-row seat. By the way, thanks for the business, you two. A lot of couples stayed for an extra bottle of wine and dessert. There was some serious romance in Rosewood *that* night!" She went to Angela's daughter and covered her ears. "At least, there was at *my* address!"

Hooting and hollering ensued. "Are all baby showers like this?" Adam asked.

"Yes," Angela said. "Trust me. I had three."

"I'm getting out of here, then," Adam said, laughing. "You guys are scaring me."

"Don't you want to wait until your mom and sister get here?" Rebecca asked. "They called and said they were running a bit late because of your nephew's soccer game."

"No," Adam said. "This isn't my scene. All these women and food and drinks and presents and—hey, wait a minute, maybe this *is* my scene."

More laughter, and then Carly called, "Adam, please, before you go, tell us the story?"

"What story?"

Carly came closer. "Rebecca told me that Molly told *her* that you two have known each other for years. Since college."

Nervousness rattled Molly from head to toe. Thankfully, if Adam was having the same feeling, it wasn't the slightest bit noticeable. "That's right," he said with complete calm.

"Suddenly you're here and you two are married, and—there has to be a great story behind that."

The room stilled into silence, waiting for a story that they had no idea would be a work of fiction.

Molly stood poised to jump in, although she had no idea what she would say if she did.

Adam looked around the room. It seemed as though he were examining each face, which Molly wasn't sure she'd be able to do if she were about to lay a big doozy of a tale on them. But Adam had the rapt attention of every single guest, and then he spoke.

"There really isn't a story, and I've wondered about that myself. I don't know how this kind of thing works. I'm not an expert on love, or feelings, or— It's just, one day, you look at someone and you realize that it's become something different, something more. You don't even know which day, or why, and that doesn't make sense to you because if your whole being has changed that much, you think you should be able to pinpoint it to the minute. Like, 'yeah, it was definitely when she said this,' or 'maybe it was when she did that,' or— But you can't. It's just changed, and you have to change, too. Even if you didn't expect it, she's suddenly what you need to be. She's your future, and you have to be in that future. You have to be in love."

Molly forgot to breathe. When Adam had begun the speech, he'd been addressing the room at large, but by the time he'd gotten to the last few words, she was the only one he was looking at. He reached out and traced a finger down her cheek.

She heard a sniffle, and it didn't come from her, and it wasn't Adam, and that's when she remembered they weren't alone. She peered around at her friends, so animated a moment ago, and now unmoving party statues, frozen while holding little crackers with cheese and champagne glasses.

Sylvia was the first one to move. She put an arm around Molly's shoulders. "You'd better get out of here," she said to Adam, "unless you want about ten more women in love with you."

Peals of laughter rang out, and noise and motion resuscitated the room.

Janine and Pam chose that moment to swing through the front door, weighed down with shopping bags full of brightly wrapped gifts. Rebecca rushed forward to welcome them and take their bags. "Hey, sis, did we miss anything good?" Janine asked Molly after kissing her cheek.

"N-no," Molly said.

"Were you surprised?" Janine pressed.

"Yes," Molly said, looking at Adam. "Very surprised." Surprised that it sounded so real. But it was an act. Just like his pretending to jump to fix the kitchen sink.

It was all a big act.

Adam slipped out the back door, throwing a wink at her before letting it slam behind him.

Though she'd just heard Adam utter the most beautiful, eloquent words she'd ever heard, and though she was surrounded with people who cared about her and were there to celebrate her happiness, Molly had never felt so depressed in her life.

Sarah Abernathy and Judith Martin lingered in a corner, leaning against a bookcase and chatting. Molly went up to them. "Did you both get cake?"

"Far more than my fair share, thanks," Sarah said. "I'm so happy for you. First the baby and then a romance with that amazing guy. You really have it all."

Molly's breath caught. If Sarah only had any idea. "Thanks," she said. "How's Justin?"

"If you see him, feel free to ask him for me," Sarah said, curling her lip. "We're on complete opposite shifts. I swear, sometimes I think that hospital tries to break up marriages for fun. I thought we'd see each other all the time."

"It'll pass," Molly said. "Last time we talked about it, your shifts were different."

"True. It's just frustrating to never get to see your own husband."

"I'm jealous," Judith cut in. "Personally, I'd be glad to see Sam once a month, get his share of the mortgage, and tell him I'd see him in another thirty days."

"Another fight?" Sarah asked, sympathetic.

"Probably still the same one you remember," Judith said. "It goes in installments, like a soap opera. Earlier today, he calls me from work, and he's got the *nerve* to tell me that—"

"Excuse me," Molly mumbled politely. She hated to leave Sarah alone with what would doubtless be a long, miserable story, but Molly had enough of her own worries tonight to take on—or even temporarily pretend to take on—someone else's. She edged around the perimeter of the room, studying the photos on the walls. They were pictures of family and friends of the Turners, the couple who owned this house and were renting it to Rebecca.

"Blair and Tom told me I could put my own pictures up on the walls," Rebecca said behind her. "But I kind of like keeping those up there, even though I have no idea who they are. It's like I have more people looking out for me."

"It must feel a little strange sometimes, living in your own place that's not really your own place."

"The whole thing is strange. Being in this house, being in the suburbs. I— Oh, that's the doorbell. Be right back. Get ready to open presents." She dashed off.

Molly wandered over to where Carly and Angela were hanging out. "Ladies," Molly said, "what's going on over here?"

"Here comes Zooey," Angela said. "She must have just arrived."

Zooey Finnegan hugged Molly with one arm, balancing two boxes in the crook of her other elbow. "Congratulations, Molly. I brought you a gift from the Lever family, and a little one from me."

"That's so sweet of you," Molly said. "Can't you stay? We'd love to have you join us."

"Rebecca already asked me, but I really can't. Jack Junior has a cold and Emily's flat-out refusing to go to bed. Jack's watching them until I get back, but he has a lot of work to do tonight and I want to make life a little easier for him. After all, that's what the nanny gets paid for." She giggled. "Have fun, you all." She left, and the three women watched her until the door closed behind her.

Rebecca joined them. "I tried to get her to stay."

"She couldn't," Molly said. "It was nice of her to drop in, though."

"I sent her home with some cake."

"Did any of you happen to notice," Carly asked, "how flustered she got the second she mentioned Jack Lever's name?"

"I did," Angela said. "But it was cute."

Molly asked the question they were all inevitably pondering. "What, you guys think there's something going on between Jack and Zooey? She works for him."

She eyed Rebecca, remembering Rebecca's interest in Jack the other day, but said nothing more, also recalling Rebecca's request to be discreet. Rebecca's gaze was bouncing back and forth between Angela and Carly, as if trying to determine which of them, if either, knew anything.

But if they did, they weren't revealing for sure. "Anything's possible," Carly said.

"Refill, anyone?" they heard.

"Me, please," Carly said, holding out her glass before she realized Megan was the one who had asked.

Megan took the glass with a small smile. "Sure. Anyone else?"

Heads shook and Megan left.

"We're gossiping," Angela said. "Technically, this is very wrong."

"We're women," Carly pointed out. "Technically, this is in our DNA."

"Besides," Molly added, "we're merely speculating about people we like. We're not engaging in spreading malicious rumors about things we know nothing about, like two women we all happen to know who will remain nameless."

"Rhonda and Irene aren't coming tonight, are they?" Carly asked.

"So much for nameless," Molly commented, but she didn't begrudge Carly in the slightest. A couple of months ago, Rhonda and Irene had crashed the Danbury Way block party and harangued Carly so much about her divorce that she had to seek sanctuary in a bathroom.

"Please. As if I'd invite them," Rebecca said. "More like, I jumped through hoops to make sure they didn't find out I was throwing this shindig at all. Enough of this. It's time for Molly to open presents."

"Presents, presents, presents," the women chanted, until the whole room joined in. Molly was guided to a big velvet armchair, where she sat surrounded with huge boxes and satiny bows.

"I think if I added up all my birthdays and doubled them, this would still be more presents than I've ever gotten in my life," Molly said.

"Leave them all here tonight and send Adam to bring them home for you tomorrow," Rebecca suggested.

Megan handed Carly her drink refill and sat on the floor at Molly's feet. "I'll mark down who gave you what," she said. "A very important duty because later, you'll never remember."

Molly pulled her pad and pen from her handbag and gave them to Megan, grateful that a list was being created. *Something* organized amid all this cheery confusion was a comfort.

She began by carefully removing tape and folding discarded wrapping paper, but after a half hour, she was tearing through like a child. After an hour, she was done, and exhausted, and had about a million things that she'd needed, as well as a million things she didn't know she needed and a million things she wasn't sure *why* she needed.

The women broke up into small groups and dove into the cake again, and Angela came over to Molly. "How are you, hon?"

"I can't believe opening presents can make someone tired, but I'm wiped out."

"It's too much stimulation," Angela said, "and it's getting late. Party's over, huh?"

Molly nodded, too weary to respond. Angela gestured with her head to the love seat in the corner, where her daughter Olivia had curled up, overcome by fun-fatigue. Megan rubbed little gentle circles on Olivia's back while she chatted with Sarah.

"Anyway, now's when you need to sleep," Angela said. "When the baby comes, it's a whole different ball game."

"That's what everyone always says," Molly said.

Angela cocked her head. "You don't believe it?"

"Oh, I do," Molly said. "It's just— See, I'm really very organized."

She was startled when Angela laughed. "Oh, I'm not laughing at you," Angela assured her. "I'm not. But once you're a mother, all organization goes right out the window and chaos reigns supreme. You're lucky if you can keep up."

Molly must have allowed her terror to show on her face, because Angela sobered. "You'll be fine. No one doubts you. You're Molly Jackson. Or— Molly Shibbs?"

"Molly Jackson."

"You're Molly Jackson of M.J. Consulting. You can handle anything. And if you can't, you hire some outside consultants. Like me, and Zooey, who knows plenty about kids by this time, and Sylvia, and Adam's family. I guarantee, none of us knew a thing before we started. It comes with experience. You'll get there."

"Mmm," Molly answered.

"Plus, you've got that nice new husband of yours," Angela said, "and I have a feeling he's not the type to let you go it alone."

"No," Molly said. "Not really."

Not yet.

Chapter Ten

Adam clicked off the Mets game highlights when he heard Molly come home. She shuffled into the living room, her hair in a damp twist, and collapsed on the sofa beside him. She didn't seem to notice that her calf had landed against his and, more alarmingly, didn't seem to care that her wet dress molded against her body and threatened to stain the thick cushions.

"That was shaping up to be a wild night," Adam said. "I'd sort of expected prim, sedate women sitting around with bows in their hair, sipping tea and nibbling finger sandwiches. Instead, it looks like you got doused with champagne."

"No," Molly answered. "It started to rain."

Adam was embarrassed at having muted the TV set every time he thought he heard a footstep, yet completely missing the rain pattering against the dry street. Now, drops streaked down the windowpane, illuminated by the streetlamp outside. "How did you get that wet in the short distance from there to here?"

"I took my time."

Adam eyeballed her. "Are you all right? Partying until after midnight, meandering around in the rain heedless of your good health."

"I was thinking."

"Bad habit," he observed. "About what?"

He didn't really know if he wanted her to say, *About your little speech earlier.* Then again, he didn't know that he didn't want her to say that.

"I haven't been to a party since—since the reunion," Molly pointed out.

Oh, great. "True," he began cautiously.

"I was thinking how ironic it was that if I hadn't gone to the reunion, tonight's party wouldn't have had a reason to happen."

Adam raised a brow. "True again. But where's this going?"

"I don't know. I started thinking about that night, and—I never said goodbye to you that night."

"No," Adam said. "You didn't. But I saw you leave."

"You saw me?"

"You and Zach."

She turned her head and let it fall back at an angle

on the sofa arm. It didn't appear very comfortable, but perhaps she was too absorbed in studying him to move. "In fact," she said, "I didn't talk to you after that night until my birthday. I was avoiding everyone because I was obviously preoccupied with being knocked up. But why were you avoiding me?"

Adam looked away from her and shrugged. He'd wished he'd left the television on, every man's universal prop for feigned nonchalance. He just stared at the dark, still-crackling screen, aware it caused him to look even guiltier.

"You *were* ducking me," Molly said. "You were mad at me because I didn't say goodbye."

"Not just for that," Adam finally said, unable to hold back. "But also because you were hanging off the arm of that lunkhead."

"Why didn't you stop me?"

"What?" Adam sat up straight and leaned over her. *"What?"*

"You should have stopped me," Molly accused.

"I should have stopped you?" Adam was incredulous. "Are you kidding? I can't stop Molly Jackson if I'm driving a tank. No one can. And as you're conveniently forgetting, I told you all through college and every wistful time you brought up Zach Jones in the years that followed that he was nothing but a slob."

"I thought you were just jealous."

"Jealous? Of what?"

"That I liked him."

Adam couldn't believe that, all along, he'd been that transparent.

"And," Molly added, "that he was so cool and successful and prepared to have it all in life."

"I'm cool," Adam protested weakly.

"And you're my friend. You should have at least tried to stop me."

"Molly," Adam said, flinging himself back against the sofa, "you're Little Miss Overachiever. You get everything you aim for in life. A part of me knew you'd get Zach, too, eventually. Standing in your way would have been a waste of my time and yours."

Molly sighed. "I guess, but—I wish someone, something had happened to make me see what a fool I was about to be."

Adam didn't go with the glib, *You can only learn from your own mistakes.*

"I went on a crash diet for about a month before that stupid reunion," Molly said. "Zach came up to me while I was standing near the dessert buffet. I couldn't believe I'd caught his attention, and then suddenly we were talking more and more, filling our plates, and I ate a mini cannoli, and that was it. It was probably because it was my first bite of sugar in thirty days and not his mesmerizing crap."

"It was him," Adam corrected her. "He dazzled you. He always did."

Molly was silent a moment. "Yeah, he did. He was

like a golden grand prize. He was smart, ambitious, driven, popular, athletic, sexy—everything I wanted."

"Everything you already were."

"I was so convinced, from that first time I saw him, that he was my kindred spirit. My destined love match."

"I told you again and again, Molly, destined love matches don't frequent freshman keg parties."

"You didn't know anything."

"So you said."

"At least, I thought you didn't. Because at the reunion, he was even more—more everything. He was the mature version of all of those qualities. A Wall Street whiz. A shining star. Before, he was merely potential, but six months ago, he was finally *it.* And he told me *I* was it, and wondering why he didn't realize it before."

Good point, Zach. Why didn't you notice it when I did? A long, long time before you...

"It all happened so fast," Molly said. "One minute I was talking to him and the next minute he was trying to unzip my dress in the hall outside the restrooms...."

Adam felt ill. "Stop right there, please."

Molly shuddered. "It makes me sick to even think about it now."

At least that was a small relief.

"We ended up at a motel a few blocks from the party. We stayed Friday night, Saturday night, and by Sunday morning, he was packing his bags and telling me what a great weekend he had. And I said—oh, I don't believe this now. I said, 'I can't wait until next weekend.' And he said, 'Why?'" She closed her eyes and turned her face to the ceiling. "He said, 'Why?' He really meant it. Then it must have been on my face, and then on *his* face I saw— God, he couldn't even be nice enough to muster up some pity. It was horror. Sheer horror, like it was occurring to him I might show up at his house and boil a bunny rabbit on his stove."

She shook her head, and kept shaking it. "He said, 'This was just fun, right?' And he kept saying it. 'Right? Right?' Until I agreed. 'Yeah. Right.' He offered to pay for another night for me so I could stay, but I would not let him walk away from me like that. I threw myself together and was out the door about five minutes later. So I would be the first to leave. So I wouldn't be the one left alone."

Adam's regret burned him from the inside out. Regret that he didn't realize this all would and could happen with a jerk like Zach. Regret that he had abandoned her and left her to deal with her hurt by herself for weeks, months.

"Not long after that, I found out that Zach had left me a parting gift," she said. "And the first thing I thought was, it's a consolation prize. A lifetime supply of Rice-A-Roni."

She smiled a sad smile. "I didn't know what to do at first. If Zach was horrified that day, I could only imagine what he'd be like when I called him with this news. I turned it over and over in my head. I never planned for a baby, not like this. Not alone, not at the height of my career, not after I just made a financial decision to buy a house. But—" She stopped and bit her lip.

"But what?" Adam gently prodded.

"I thought, who would be fool enough to turn down a lifetime supply of Rice-A-Roni? It may not be the prize I set out to win, but maybe it's what I needed all along." She sighed. "I'm thirty-two. My eggs aren't getting any younger and spousal candidates were not flocking to my door. Not at that point, anyway," she said, nudging Adam with her foot.

He caught her foot and eased her sandal off. Her skin felt cool from the rain. He didn't rub, well aware of her epic ticklishness. He just held her bare foot.

"I want this baby so badly," Molly said. "He or she will be so beyond worth what I went through. I just wish I didn't have to have the embarrassing sour memory of how it happened. I was so stupid," she added, almost in a whisper. "I was duped into believing my dream man was possible, and that he was it. I hated Zach for that. I hated that he tricked me into thinking he was something that he isn't.

"Now," she said, "I'm doing the same thing. You and I. The same exact thing. We're tricking everyone about our marriage. We're the dupers this time around."

"This is different," Adam said. "This is for your own greater good, for the baby. Not to hurt anyone."

As soon as the words were out of his mouth, Adam realized that he, for one, was hurting already, and in for a lot more.

"After this baby is born, after this year is over," Molly said, "I will never lie again. This baby will have nothing but the straight-up truth forever."

They sat together on the sofa, unmoving, for a very long time. The streetlight on the curb outside the window blew its bulb, drawing them deeper into the night.

"I'm sorry I didn't stop you," Adam said finally.

She didn't respond, and Adam thought she had fallen asleep until she said groggily, "I'm sorry I wouldn't have let you."

They both faded into slumber, and with Adam's last remaining conscious strength, he tried to push away Molly's past pain and his future pain to languish in the warm present moment.

Molly read the e-mail twice, to make sure she wasn't imagining its strange contents. It was from Jean-Luc Klinsman, one of the ALCOP associates who'd interviewed her right before Pieter Tilberg. Jean-Luc wrote that he and Tilberg were going to be in Rosewood tomorrow taking a final look at the plant and meeting with numerous contractors, and since Molly lived right in town, would she like to accompany them to dinner?

Naturally, Jean-Luc added, her husband was invited, as well.

Molly, usually astute when it came to employers' motives, wondered what to make of this unexpected development. As it happened, she did have some initial implementation plans to review with her new boss, but this sounded more like a social occasion. It baffled her. She'd have thought he hired her because it was foolish not to, because she was the most qualified, but that it likely wasn't something he'd particularly wanted to do, and that definitely he wouldn't meet with her any more than necessary.

He believed she *had* a husband, right? He must have background-checked her by now. Maybe he just wanted—who knew what he wanted?

Maybe he just wanted to be nice?

Hmm.

If she couldn't figure out Tilberg's motive, she could at least formulate her own motive. Spin this social opportunity to her advantage somehow.

Her spine stiffened as an idea lit up. Then she winced as a stab of lower back pain forced her to relax again.

They could come here. She'd make dinner for them. That way she remained on her own turf. Besides, Tilberg, in traveling back and forth between Utrecht and New York State quite often, probably ate in a restaurant or hotel every night. It would be the kind thing to make him a home-cooked meal. She'd do it for anyone.

Her hands hovered over the keyboard as her mind twisted the idea around every angle. Would it give

Tilberg the opposite impression that she was going for? Make him think she was only a happy, kitchen-bound housewife with a little consulting job on the side?

No, he'd hired her based on her stellar résumé and, besides, she was proud of her newly decorated home. Of course, she wouldn't be able to tell him the thing she liked most about it—that she'd bought it herself—but she still thought the home would be a positive asset to show off. And maybe it would warm Tilberg to her a little more as a person, which was never a bad move in creating a professional relationship.

Besides, she would have access to all her files here, so if dinner conversation did indeed turn into shoptalk, she could retrieve whatever she needed from her office.

She picked up the phone, spun her Rolodex around and dialed.

"Gibraltar Foods, Adam Shibbs."

Molly smiled in spite of herself. She couldn't help it. Adam's professional greeting couldn't mask his real self. She could hear the perpetual grin on his face.

The smile disappeared almost as quickly as she considered the performance they were going to have to put on for their guests. The elaborate show of a loving, together couple, and not of two in-over-their-heads best friends merely married on paper who maybe did share two amazing, memorable kisses that may have changed her forever but…

"Anyone there?" Adam said.

She cleared her throat. "Hey, it's me."

"Hi, *me.* Slacking off on the job, eh?"

"Hardly, Shibbs."

Oh, Misgiving City. It wasn't too late to put the kibosh on this idea. But what had Adam said that first day in her home? *The three of us will pull this off.*

Then she remembered one more thing—that incredible soliloquy that had left the women of Danbury Way in uncharacteristic, stunned silence. Adam could do this. If he could, she damn well could, too.

"Can you keep tomorrow night open?" she asked.

"I keep every night open, with the only caveat that it's going to be for something fun."

Molly rolled her eyes. "Oh, fun doesn't begin to describe the night we're going to have. Trust me."

"Intriguing," he answered. "What's up?"

"I'll tell you later."

They hung up and Molly hit Reply on Jean-Luc's e-mail.

Jean-Luc, Thank you so much for the generous invitation, but may I suggest you and Mr. Tilberg come to my home for dinner? I'd be happy to pick you up at your hotel at whatever time is convenient. I look forward to—

Suddenly, she stopped typing, squinted at the screen, and deleted several sentences back. Then she amended— May I suggest you and Mr. Tilberg come to our home for dinner? I'd be happy to pick you up at your hotel. We— Molly deleted again. My husband and I look forward to having you.

She stared at the words, knowing they'd come from her, but they read like a foreign language. She cocked her head. A pretty foreign language, like French. But still foreign.

She hit Send before she could change her mind. Then she clicked open an empty document, and began to create a list of recipes, ingredients, other things to buy later. This was perfect. More work. She couldn't be happier. More work would distract her from thinking about the way Adam's voice had melted around the word "intriguing," and from thinking about what else she could intrigue him with if she was so inclined.

She exhaled. More work. *That's* what she loved. She ignored her back twinges and the beads of sweat on her forehead. She rubbed at her dry, grainy eyes and focused on the new task at hand.

The next afternoon, Adam was rehearsing quietly in his cubicle. "Yes, we love this house. We can't wait for the baby to come."

He took a deep breath. "Thank you very much for dropping by to see us."

"You're welcome," he heard behind him, as a young administrative assistant dropped a manila envelope into his in-box. She glanced around his desk area and, finding him alone, shrugged with a bemused expression and moved on.

Perhaps he ought to also rehearse loving gazes at his pregnant wife, but unfortunately, he was pretty sure his were already convincing. Transparent.

The phone made him jump. "Gibraltar Foods, Ada—"

"Adam, we are in crisis mode. DEFCON one."

Molly's tone was calm, but it was a practiced professional calm, the kind of demeanor they teach you to adopt in business school when your six million-dollar deal is crumbling down all around you.

"Are you all right? The baby?"

"It's not me. It's the oven. It's broken."

"What?" Adam was flummoxed. "Didn't we use it yesterday?"

"Yes," Molly said, a hint of impatience crawling through. "I tried everything. I also called a repair person, who can get here Friday at the very earliest."

"I don't suppose we can reschedule."

"No, Tilberg is in town today." She paused. "Between us, I'm trying very hard not to freak out."

"You're doing a top-notch job. Remember what the doctor told you. No stress. Maybe we should cancel."

"We'll have to take them to a restaurant after all," she said, not hearing or simply ignoring his last suggestion. "This is going to make me look like an idiot, but there's no alternative."

"You couldn't help it."

"That's not the point."

"Right," Adam said. "Uh, one more thing. I'm going to be late tonight."

"Oh, no, I don't believe this—"

"No, not really late, just a little bit late. I have a conference call I can't miss. Pick up Tilberg and his guy at their hotel, and I'll be home by the time you get back."

"All right."

"Listen, don't tell them about the oven."

"Adam, what are you talking about? I have to."

"No, I have a better idea. Let me tell them when you get back home."

"Why?"

"Because," he explained. "Your relationship with this company is brand-new. Do you really want to have them hear bad news out of your own mouth in your first face-to-face after you've been hired? Let me tell them. It's a little detail, but I think every detail contributes to your image at this phase. They should hear only positive things from you as long as you can help it."

He could hear Molly thinking it over. "All right," she said somewhat grudgingly. "You actually make sense."

"Very occasionally, it happens that I do," Adam said. "Relax. It'll be fine. I'll meet you at the house."

He hung up, and eyeballed his day planner. Just as he thought. His next conference call was two weeks away.

He called the front desk. "I need to knock off a

little early today," he said. Then he yanked open his desk and rifled through a battered stack of business cards until he found the one he needed.

Adam heard his wife and their two guests enter the house just as he lit the last candle. Soft jazz echoed through the house—Molly had quite a sound system, one that he suspected she was as unfamiliar with as she was with her television.

He straightened his tie, something he never did. He tended to let the knot go slacker and slacker throughout the workday before he tore it off in the car on his commute home. Now, it felt tight, constraining and perfectly impressive.

"Adam!" Molly called, and Adam swung out of the kitchen into the living room.

He extended his hand to the nearest man. "Welcome."

"Thank you," he said. "I'm Jean-Luc Klinsman. A pleasure to meet you, Mr. Jackson."

"Oh, it's Shibbs," he corrected smoothly. "Molly's kept her business name. Or else she would have had to change M.J. Consulting to—M.S. Consulting," he realized out loud. He elbowed Molly. "Ha. Ms. Consulting."

Molly's scary glare was brief, almost subliminal, but effective. Adam shut up.

Jean-Luc chuckled at Adam's joke as the second man stepped forward. "I'm Pieter Tilberg," he said.

His voice was neutral and cool, but Adam suspected meanness wasn't behind it. Maybe nervousness. He may have been an influential, wealthy businessman, but he was still a guest in a relative stranger's home in a country other than his own.

"Something smells wonderful," Jean-Luc commented, and Adam saw Molly's eyebrows push together as she lifted her chin and sniffed the air.

"Uh, yes…" she said. "Something, um, does?"

Adam gestured into the dining room. "I've kept Molly's wonderful meal warm. Can I get you gentlemen some wine?"

The men entered the room with appreciative murmurs, and Molly pushed in behind them. When she saw the spread on the table, her mouth dropped open. A tureen filled with a beautiful butternut squash soup sat beside a huge platter—the platter she'd bought to entertain but hadn't yet used. Now it held a crown roast, surrounded with new potatoes. A bowl of fresh green beans completed the spread. Her plain clear glass dinnerware sparkled against the buttercup tablecloth. Her golden Murano glass bottle held fat, startling pink and orange Gerbera daisies.

Adam grinned. He had to admit, it was a good-looking dinner. Being in the food industry, he knew several caterers that could do this and do it fast. The only hard part was choosing one. Karen Reiner was a whiz, and he'd sent her off about fifteen minutes ago with a generous and grateful tip.

He poured three glasses of red wine from the already-opened bottle, and poured seltzer for Molly, who was still staring around the room in too-obvious shock.

"Are you all right, babe?" Adam asked, encircling her waist with his arm. "You can't possibly be tired. You never get tired."

He said it loud enough for Tilberg to hear, and Molly smiled. "That's true. I'm simply—proud of dinner."

They sat down and Adam saw her gaze roam over the china cabinet, where he'd rearranged a few things to prominently display in frames a few pictures of he and Molly he'd located around her home. Grinning under identical ski caps on the slopes in junior year, noses chapped bright red from the wind. Toasting each other at a wedding party table where they were paired when Molly's former roommate wed a friend of his five years ago. At a New Year's party, Molly laughing into the camera with a tiara on her head proclaiming "2000" and Adam smiling also, but his head turned to the side, looking only at her.

That photo had given him pause in the midst of his frenzied dinner preparations. If he weren't him, if he were some random observer, he'd say that guy in the picture had it bad.

How could he have been so ignorant of his own feelings for so long? Or was it that he'd been merely unable to articulate them to himself? He'd refused commitment with any and all women since freshman year, since meeting Molly had created standards he'd never needed before.

Molly gasped, and Adam turned. "This is *really* delicious," she said around a mouthful.

"If you do say so yourself," Adam reminded her.

"Oh, right, if I do say so myself," Molly followed along. "Because, after all, I did cook this all up. Myself."

She was a terrible liar.

She was a fantastic woman.

Adam swallowed, even though he hadn't yet sampled any food. "Mr. Tilberg, what made you choose Rosewood for ALCOP's expansion?"

The four of them slipped into conversation that began as stilted and formal, but lightened as stomachs were satisfied and glasses were refilled. Adam eventually loosened his tie, then put his arm around Molly's shoulders.

She was hyperalert of every touch that passed between her and Adam, deliberate or incidental. She responded to his affection with her own without the difficulty she fully expected, placing her hand in his, brushing a finger against his cheek, exchanging a lingering look. In this part of their charade, she didn't feel deceitful, even though she was supposed to. It was honest and…real.

Adam winked at her and cleared her plate along with their guests'.

Oh, God. This was real.

The shock of discovery had to be all over her face. Trying to concentrate on a story that Jean-Luc was relating, she lifted her hands to her cheeks and rubbed her skin. She peeked through her fingers at Tilberg. Although he'd visibly relaxed, he wasn't quite as animated as the rest of the table. He appeared to be examining the room, taking in details.

Molly wouldn't even have noticed, if she didn't truly have a secret to hide.

Adam came back into the room. "Are you married, Mr. Tilberg?"

"No," he said. "I have not yet met a woman to keep up with me."

Molly raised her eyebrows, wondering if Tilberg was aware of his own reputation, and how it must surely affect his dating life, if nothing else.

Adam chuckled. "I think you've now met a woman who can keep up with you. Too bad for you, I saw her first." He kissed Molly's cheek, and as he drew his lips away, Molly felt the spot flush.

"You have known each other a long time," Tilberg said, and not as a question. He nodded toward the pictures, and Molly realized her hunch was correct.

"Yes," she said. "But it took me nearly that long to convince Adam that I was the one."

"I knew right away," Adam protested. "But it was more fun to make you chase me."

Molly punched him in the arm, maybe a little bit harder than jest.

Jean-Luc laughed. "Then you must tell us how it happened that you finally caught him," he cajoled.

"Oh, that can't be an interesting story for you," Molly said, trying in desperation to brush it off.

"Why do you assume that?" Tilberg asked, tilting his glass for a sip and swallowing. "We are stodgy businessmen who can't appreciate a love story?"

"N-no," Molly said, barely controlling her stammer. "Of course not. I meant—"

"No, please, I am only teasing you," Tilberg said, "but we should truly like to hear."

Molly looked around and saw the dinner, the photos, the flickering candles casting shadows on the three men's faces. She saw her home in this new light, infused with new potential and energy, and she saw her best friend's devotion spread out in front of her. Her chest filled with realization.

Adam shifted in his seat, a subtle sign that he was going to take care of Tilberg's request, but before he could speak, Molly cut in, "Honey, let me." She peered at her husband through her lashes. "I think I can speak for both of us on this one."

Adam swallowed. Molly took control of the room.

She turned to Tilberg and Jean-Luc. "It would be easier to tell you a simple love story, but this was much more of a slow, subtle evolution. We were friends since we were kids in college. We grew up into adults before each other's eyes, winding our way into each other's lives. We—I woke up one morning and realized love wasn't happening, but instead, it had already happened at some magical point I couldn't begin to identify."

Molly discovered it wasn't a struggle to remember Adam's own words from the baby shower, because they had been the same words already caught in her heart. She released them now, to finally confess that at the center of their elaborate deception was a pulsing core of honesty and reality that she couldn't ignore anymore.

She laid her hand over the top of Adam's, and spoke her truth to him, steady and clear. "It just changed, and I had to change, too. Even if I didn't expect it—or plan it—he was suddenly what I needed to be. I had to be in that future. I had to be in love."

Without a muscle moving or an eyelash twitching, Adam's face transformed, brightened. He searched her eyes, his gaze going from one to the other, as if trying and failing to find a sign that would give away that this was all still a hoax. Finding none, his smile widened, the outside corners of those impossible green eyes creasing. Molly, dimly aware of their small audience, fought the urge to smooth her finger along the grooves.

"Time for dessert," she whispered. Then she quirked her eyebrows. Was there dessert? "Maybe?" she asked.

"There's always dessert," Adam said. "It's the most fun part, and in the end, you have to give in even if you didn't want to."

Molly nodded, and turned to see Tilberg discreetly slipping Jean-Luc a handkerchief as he watched her and Adam. "I apologize," Molly said as Adam headed to the kitchen. "I didn't mean to turn this into a—personal moment."

"We all but asked you to," Tilberg said.

"It's fine," Jean-Luc said, dabbing at his eyes. "Pardon me. My allergies are acting up."

"I get them, too," she assured the younger associate.

Adam carried out a delicate silver serving tray that Molly had never used. Her parents had given it to her as a housewarming gift, telling her it would be lovely to use when entertaining clients, but Molly, preferring to keep her clients—and maybe most people?—at arm's distance, hadn't had the opportunity. Adam laid down the tray and she heard Tilberg exclaim, "Ah!"

She looked at him, puzzled to see him staring at the contents of the tray with undisguised pleasure.

Molly examined "her" dessert, and found she couldn't even identify the little round pancake-type pastries. Hoping her guests wouldn't pry for the recipe, she glanced at Tilberg again, but his eyes were glowing and he was smiling. Real smiling, with teeth showing, even. *This* guy.

"Mr. Tilberg?" Molly prompted.

"*Poffertjes,*" he said.

"Sorry?" Molly asked, baffled.

"*Poffertjes,*" he repeated. "I have not had these

in…a very long time. My father used to prepare them for my brothers and myself, when we all lived in the same home." He shook his head in wonder. "I did not even know they had them in America."

Molly chanced a look at Adam, who crinkled his eyes happily. "Luckily, the Internet makes so much possible," he said, nudging Molly. "Especially a simple Dutch recipe."

"Right," she agreed, grabbing Adam's hand and lacing her fingers with his.

"This is how we ate it, too," Tilberg said. "With butter and icing."

"I've only had them several times," Jean-Luc said, "but never on this side of the Atlantic. Wonderful."

Tilberg spoke directly to Molly. "What a treat, for you to do this for us. Thank you, Molly."

"You're—you're welcome," Molly said, dishing the *poffertjes* out to all of them. "I aim to please." As soon as she filled her own small dessert plate, she popped one of the *poffertjes* in her mouth, and sighed at how fluffy it was. She rolled her tongue around the sugar. Then she caught Adam watching her—or rather, watching her mouth. Without batting an embarrassed eyelash, she poked her tongue out and captured a small dollop of butter there. She put another pastry in her mouth, and watched Adam right back, checking that he clearly interpreted the promises she intended to fulfill before tonight came to an end.

"*I'm* pleased," Adam said, and Molly was glad their guests were too absorbed in their light dessert to notice the heavy innuendo.

Molly fit tin foil over the last of the *poffertjes* and handed the plate to Tilberg.

"Are you sure?" her best client asked with a grin, shrugging on his suit coat. "You don't think the baby might crave to have more?"

Molly marveled at the genuine delight on this man's face, and that he believed she was responsible. She didn't feel too guilty for this particular fib. There were far worse untruths in the world than one that could make a person so happy.

"No one goes home empty-handed," Molly insisted. "Or, rather, to the hotel."

"Get room service to bring you some maple syrup in the morning and have yourself a breakfast," Adam suggested.

"I'm sorry," Molly said to Tilberg and his associate, "that we never got a chance to discuss my plans for—"

Tilberg held up a hand. "Plenty of time," he said, "on the clock. Jean-Luc will schedule a meeting with you for next week. We will be back in Rosewood by Monday."

Molly didn't bother to ponder again what led Tilberg to invite her to dinner in the first place. The night ended up well, and that was all she cared about.

She peeked over her shoulder at Adam. Well, *almost* all she cared about. Right now, she also cared about decreasing the number of people in her house—and increasing the privacy.

The cab she'd called stopped at the curb, and they all proceeded to shake hands, though much warmer than several hours ago. As Adam clapped Jean-Luc on the shoulder and they exchanged parting soccer references, Tilberg grasped Molly's hand in both his own.

"Thank you again," he said.

"Anytime you're in town," Molly answered, squeezing. "Honestly. This was fun."

Adam put his arm around Molly's waist as Tilberg relinquished her hand and held up his dessert plate. "A very beautiful thing to see," he said, but he was looking at his host and hostess, not at the dessert. "Good night."

The men left and as soon as the cab made a U-turn and sped off in perpetual cablike hurry, Molly closed the door and whirled to face Adam. "*Poffertjes?*"

"Not from the caterer," Adam confirmed, slowly approaching her. "She brought everything else. I did some quick online research, then called a bakery I know that specializes in unusual desserts. They whipped me up a batch in record time."

He backed Molly up against the wall and brought his face inches from hers.

"What you just did for me—for us—for them," Molly began.

"Yes?" His breath was sugar.

"It was a staggering feat to pull off."

"Yeah," Adam said. "Can I assume that it all met with your satisfaction?"

Molly chose her words. "You did well," she replied, "but regrettably, I'm still far from satisfied."

Adam lowered his mouth until his lips just barely touched hers. "You're a hell of a lot of work, Molly Jackson," he said against her mouth.

He darted his tongue out and touched the center of her top lip, and she shuddered with the eroticism of the tiny touch.

"However," he added, "I'm sure you'll find I'm the most skilled man for this very delicate job."

"You're hired," Molly breathed. "I need you to start right away."

Adam acquiesced by pulling out the clip in her hair, and wound both hands into her released curls. He pushed his mouth against hers and she tasted the evening's second helping of dessert.

Chapter Eleven

Molly yanked off her silvery lace shirt and tossed it over Adam's shoulder while he reached behind her and unhooked her bra. A moment later, it joined her shirt on the floor. Molly deftly unraveled the knot of Adam's tie and slid the silk out from under his starched collar. She unbuttoned him from the neck down, stopping to lick each inch of newly exposed skin. She dipped her tongue into his navel, and his stomach clenched. When she peered up at him, he was laughing.

"Funny, huh?" she asked, undoing the last button and lapping the tight skin of his lower abdomen.

"Ticklish," he gasped, and Molly chuckled. Her

chin brushed the top of his pants, and she unfastened that top button as well, peeling down the band of his boxers a few centimeters with her pinky and licking one more stroke.

He gasped and his fingers twisted tighter in her hair. She let the waistband snap back and stood, letting him push his shirt down and away from them.

Desperate to feel his skin on hers, she wrapped her arms around his back and pushed against him, but the swell of her belly impeded her. She stepped slightly to the right and pulled Adam down on a diagonal angle to her, pressing into him, her breasts flattening onto his chest, her nipples hard and aching.

They both moaned, and the unfamiliar, sexy sound emanating from this man she thought she knew so well frightened her a little bit, but turned her on so exponentially greater that the trepidation was easily pushed aside.

Adam bent over and caught a nipple in his mouth, laving, suckling, playing with his tongue until she grabbed his hand and guided it between her legs. The heat of his palm inflamed her. The caress of his fingertips made her half-insane.

Ignoring her cry of protest, he slid his hand down her thigh and cupped the backs of her knees, lifting her into his arms in a swift, sure motion. He headed to the stairs.

"I wouldn't if I were you," Molly murmured. "A hernia could be in your future."

"Perhaps, but not from this," he said in her ear. "You weigh nothing, and that already defies the laws of physics because to me, you're everything."

She curled her head into his chest when he reached her bedroom and slid in sideways through the door frame, and he set her down on the bed. He stood over her and unzipped his trousers, kicking them toward the open door. He unzipped her pants and began tugging them down.

"Oh," Molly said, trying to see through the haze of need and want into her old world of reason and logic. "Maybe we can't do this…."

"I can do this," Adam assured her. "And I'm pretty sure you can, so why can't we do it together?" He eased her pants over her knees.

"No, no, I mean, the baby, and I don't know how to do it…"

"With you on top," Adam said, sliding her panties down, pausing only to dip his finger inside her.

She gasped for air through her open mouth. "How- oh, don't stop—how do you know that?"

"Research."

She fought her own urges, reached down and clasped his wrist, stopping his hand from pleasuring her. "Wait. What?"

"In your own books," Adam said, undaunted by his captured hand. He leaned down and tongue-stroked her core, once, twice. "The books you painstakingly highlighted and marked with sticky notes.

Strange, though," he said, licking her once more and listening to her answering groan before continuing. "The sex pages in your pregnancy books were pristine and crisp, like you didn't even read them."

She clasped the top of his head with her free hand, the strands of his blond hair slipping through her grasp like sand. "I didn't anticipate needing that—oh, oh—that information."

"Neither did I," he said, raising his head and kissing a trail to the top of her belly. He rested his chin on it and regarded her from under lust-heavy eyelids. "Good thing for both of us, I simply happen to be a curious guy. A collector of interesting knowledge."

He vaulted onto the bed beside her, bouncing them both up and down. "And now," he said, kissing her neck, "things have definitely gotten interesting."

Molly rolled away from him, pushed herself up and straddled him, hovering over him. She let her gaze travel the length of his body, even turning around to see his strong legs stretched out behind her. He was beautiful.

"You're beautiful," he said. His eyes had darkened with desire, now the deep green of a forest at night.

She lowered herself onto him, slowly, slowly, slowly, until the shock of her body melting into his overcame her and she exploded hard and bright just from the first moment of intimate contact. She arched her back and cried out from the release, her knees pushing into the mattress, her hands squeezing Adam's.

When she let her head drop down again, her hair tumbled forward and obscured her vision. Adam gathered it all up in a bunch and pushed it over one shoulder. He ran his hand down the other side of her bare neck and down her arm, and began to move under her, gently at first, but increasing in strength. Molly rode his rocking hips, thrusting herself against him in rhythm until she felt the tightness building inside her again, running through her limbs, swirling in her abdomen. She braced her hands on Adam's chest and their bodies, their cries synchronized until they climaxed together, his throbbing inside her, her throbbing against him.

Her hand slipped across his chest, both of them slick with sweat. She lost her balance and landed with her elbow on the inside of his bicep. "Oh!" she said as she landed. "Are you okay?"

He began to laugh, and it was Adam Shibbs's laugh, but instead of seeing it and hearing it, for the first time she also felt it, his torso shaking beneath her. "Yeah. What about you?"

"I'm fine. Sorry." But she cracked up also.

"No, it was the right thing," Adam said. "Otherwise, it would have been way too perfect and I would have been sitting here trying to convince myself this wasn't all a big Technicolor dream of fulfilling a longtime desire."

"Longtime?" she asked, propping her head up on her hand. "Really?"

"As if you didn't know."

"I didn't," she said. "I couldn't have, because then I—" She stopped. What would she have done, years ago, if she suspected he wanted her? Jumped him? No, she wouldn't have let herself, because she had a prototype, and he didn't fit it at all.

"It's okay," Adam said, somehow reading her mind. "Remember what Sylvia said? Things happen in the order they're supposed to. It wasn't time for us before. Now it is."

She raised herself up on her hands again to untangle them, then slid beside him and curled into his body.

"Molly," he mumbled into her hair. "That was the most incredible lovemaking I've ever shared. So good, in fact, that I'm strongly considering requesting a repeat performance."

"Too late," Molly assured him, and kissed his lips softly. "I'm beating you to it."

"You always were more efficient," he said.

When Adam called in late to Gibraltar Foods the next morning, he had an unfamiliar twinge of work-ethic guilt that he was sure had to be Molly's influence.

Then again, he had a sore back, a swollen mouth and a remarkable satiation that was Molly's influence also.

He glanced at the blank spot on the nightstand. At 8:00 a.m., Molly's alarm had buzzed and before he could do anything, her arm had reached out and slapped the clock facedown to the floor with a startling smash. She didn't even flinch. Instead, she'd dropped that arm across his chest, turned her back to her door—and the hallway leading to her office—and fell asleep again.

Apparently, his influence carried at least as much weight around here.

He sighed with content. There would have to be no relationship talk, no dancing around each other's feelings, no wondering where things were headed. They were already married, so the happily-ever-after part was all that remained, right? They could influence each other for many years to come, and that was perfect, in Adam's point of view.

A few hours and a bonus morning session later, Molly lay in his arms, giggling.

"Remember when we first met?" he asked. "At that lecture by some business mogul. I don't even remember his name now."

"I don't think you knew his name then," Molly pointed out. "I actually talked to you because you sat next to me. I was impressed because you went out of your way to attend the evening lecture."

"Turned out I was only there to meet girls."

"I know. And in four years, you joined the yearbook staff, played co-ed badminton and took ballroom dancing, all to meet girls."

"Pretty clever, eh?"

"Pretty obvious, I'd say."

"You liked me."

"I was hard-pressed to figure out why we were friends," she said.

"Not me. You had a cute butt. Even if you did walk around most of the time with a stick right up—"

"Don't say it," Molly warned, but with a grin.

"We were supposed to be friends," Adam said. "I didn't question it."

"Me, either, after a while." She paused. "What about now?"

"What do you mean?"

"What are we supposed to be?"

"Exactly what we are," he said. "Two people enjoying life and each other. Pardon me," he corrected, rubbing her stomach. "Three people." He cleared his throat. "Molly?"

"Mmm?"

"When are you planning on telling Zach about the baby?"

His inquiry was met with silence. After a few moments, he realized she wasn't just thinking it over. She simply wasn't responding. He nudged her shoulder. "Moll? What is it?"

"I'm not sure," she said. "Either it's that you brought that man's name up while we're in bed, or that I thought you knew full well I'm going to keep him oblivious about this baby until approximately the end of time."

"You can't do that," he protested.

She turned and gave him a sharp look. "I can't do *what?*"

"You shouldn't do that," Adam tried. "I mean, for the baby's sake."

"Everything I've done in the last six-months-plus has been for the baby's sake. That includes marrying you."

"But the baby has a right to know her—or his—father at some point, don't you think?"

Molly began, "But you're—" and then she stopped, and Adam watched her face turn from softness to stone in less than two seconds. "I see," she said, pulling away from him and sitting up. She wrapped the sheet around her body, her beautiful lush body.

"No, I have a sinking feeling you don't see," Adam said, "or else you wouldn't be angry with me. I'm not thinking about us."

"Clearly, that was my mistake."

"What?" he asked, but she stood up and yanked the sheet with her. It slid off the bed, exposing him, and she walked, half tripping over it twice, to her small bathroom and shut herself inside.

"What was your mistake?" Adam called, pulling on a pair of boxers.

"Where should I even start?" she shouted back.

"Molly," he said, "doesn't Zach have the right to get to know his baby, regardless of what happened between you?"

She stepped out of the bathroom, where she'd found a gray cotton jogsuit to put on. Her hair was wild around her head. "I think," she said, low and dangerous, "that instead of worrying about the rights Zach Jones doesn't have, you should concern yourself with the rights *you* don't have. Like the right to tell me what to do with my life and how to be a mother. Like the right to share my bed."

She was shaking. The zipper pull on her half-open hoodie rattled.

"Molly," he said, "take it easy."

"What gave you the thought at all," Molly nearly shrieked, "that I might bring Zach in on this? On us?"

"You did," he said, at a fraction of her decibel. "When you said that after this baby was born, you'd never lie again. That your baby was entitled to the truth."

Faced with her own contradiction, Molly stood there, her fists balled up, her fingers turning white.

"Please don't do this," Adam said. "Please relax. It's your decision, and I will respect it. I shouldn't have said anything, ever, and especially not this morning."

"No," she said, choking in the back of her throat and starting over. "I suppose you should have waited at least until Sunday night to tell me this was all just fun. Right? Right?"

Adam shuddered at the memory of her story about the weekend with Zach, the echoing of what he had said to her. "It's not like that, and you know it."

"I'm out of here," she said, and his heart broke that she was reacting the same way, insisting on being the one to leave.

She clattered down the steps, and while she couldn't move very fast, she stomped each step for emphasis. Adam followed her. "You can't go anywhere. Not like this. You have to relax."

At the bottom of the stairs, Molly whirled and jabbed a finger in his chest. "If there's one thing I never want to hear again," she said, "it's you telling me to relax!"

She yanked open the front door. "I don't know how I thought I could pretend for a year!" she yelled. "Because I can't pretend for even five more minutes! This fictional marriage is over!"

She slammed the front door so hard, Adam thought he heard it crack from top to bottom.

But maybe that was just his heart.

Molly's last word was still echoing in her own ears as she slammed the door behind her and looked up to find Rhonda standing at the end of her walk, staring at her with an odd expression on her face. Molly walked toward her, and would have bulldozed right through her if Rhonda hadn't sidestepped her at the last second.

"Oh, Molly," she cooed insincerely, "is there anything I can do?"

Molly pivoted, and knew without a shadow of a doubt that Rhonda had heard a lot. The living room windows had been wide open.

"Yes," she said, advancing on Rhonda and forcing

the woman to take two steps back. "In fact, there is something you can do. You can pull your cell phone out of your Kate Spade knockoff bag, and call everyone you know. Go ahead. Get the gossip express moving."

Molly turned her back on wide-eyed Rhonda and lurched down the street. She passed all the houses on idyllic Danbury Way, owned by people who would all have heard about her sham marriage by this time tomorrow.

Molly turned a corner, and another, down a long side street she'd never had occasion to pass down. She staggered a little bit, but didn't stop. Some logical part of her was aware she couldn't go far without her keys, wallet or cell phone. But the logical part was being shouted down by the emotional, overwrought part. She didn't need a destination, only her determination to get away from herself.

How could she have been so foolish *again?* Encircled in Adam's warm embrace all night, she'd dreamed about the baby, and she woke up believing that Adam wanted to be a permanent part of the baby's life. But not a moment too soon, he was pushing her in the direction of the biological father. A much more subtle approach to rejection than Zach's, but a rejection all the same.

Molly broke out in a sweat, but she was feeling cold, even as the balmy late-morning breeze should have warmed her. She smelled flowers, but she never could identify them by scent alone. The air was thick with its perfume, and her stomach lurched. She clapped a hand over her nose and mouth.

She walked even faster, trying to force her feet to keep up with the frantic pace of her racing brain.

Pro: When I kick Adam out, I don't have to see his socks next to mine in the laundry anymore. Con: I don't want him to go. Oh, God, I'm still so stupid, because I love him.

Darkness shrouded the list in her mind. She cried out even before she doubled over, as if she'd known the pain would be next, as if she'd anticipated the hurt all along.

Adam drove slowly up and down the neighboring streets, searching the sidewalk. She was a pregnant woman who left on foot. How far could she possibly have gotten?

But then, she was Molly. Even without her purse, she could be halfway to Turkey by now.

He glanced at his rearview mirror and saw only his own worried eyebrows. Speaking of turkey.

Elmer barked once, twice, scratching on the passenger window. Adam lowered the window, assuming he just wanted to put his doggy head out into the wind, but Elmer leaned out of the car as far as he could without tumbling onto the moving pavement, and barked at something. Someone.

Adam screeched to a stop at the curb, and she was

there, huddled at the curb in a ball, one arm around her middle and the other cradling her head.

He leaped out of the car and put himself under Molly, supporting her weight.

"Don't feel well," she said.

"You'll be okay," Adam said. "We're going to the hospital."

He helped Molly into the front seat as Elmer panted beside him on the sidewalk, wagging his tail, happy they'd found their friend and clueless as to anything being really wrong. Adam opened the back door and ushered Elmer into the backseat. He ran around the car to his own side and buckled himself in.

"Dad," he said, straining to hear the approaching sirens. "It's going to be all right."

"I love you, Adam. I'm sorry."

"I love you," Molly whispered. "I'm sorry."

Adam slammed his foot down on the gas.

"Don't worry, Dad."

"Don't worry," he said. "We'll get through this."

He tore through the side streets to the main road, and merged onto the parkway. "The three of us," he said.

"Stress," the doctor declared.

Molly didn't look surprised, Adam noticed. But she did appear relieved, as if she'd dreaded a worse diagnosis.

For Adam, stress *was* the one thing he never wanted to hear.

"Molly," Dr. Bristol said, "I told you last week when you came to see me that you have to cut down on your stress. And it's gotten worse. It will affect your blood pressure and more. We were lucky this time."

Molly nodded.

"But," Dr. Bristol continued, "simply being conscious of stress factors hasn't been enough. You're going to have to make some serious lifestyle changes for the rest of your pregnancy in order to cut out the stress. I don't know whether it's your job, or family issues, or worries about the baby..."

"Or all three," Adam muttered. Molly shot him a look.

"I'm happy to advise you any way I can," the doctor said, waiting until Molly turned back to him before going on. "Whatever is causing you to have panic attacks has to stop. It's putting you at risk. I'm not keeping you overnight this time, but you get right back here if anything like this happens again."

He left Adam and Molly alone, pulling the curtain around them for privacy. Molly stayed perched on the edge of the examining table, appearing frail in the paisley hospital gown. She fingered one of the tie strings hanging loose at her side.

"Well," she said, curling her toes under her socks, "at least it's not serious."

Adam froze. "Not serious?"

"You heard him. Just stress," she said. "Everyone

has stress. It's like a catchall phrase for life. If you're breathing, you're stressed. No one can help stress."

"I can."

"Well, you're the only one."

"No, *you're* the only one."

"Excuse me?"

"You're the only one," Adam said, his back teeth grinding together, "that thrives on that crazy feeling that people want to get away from and take vacations to escape. I'm not the anomaly here. I'm not the strange creature. You are. You think this is normal. This," he said, gesturing around them at the curtain, the table, the blood pressure machine in the corner, "is not normal. This is where you end up when you're not okay."

"Adam, I'll be careful. All I meant was, it's easy for the doctor to advise me to change my lifestyle but I can't make a good future for the baby sitting around on my behind." She shrugged. "I'll try to keep calm. I'll be all right."

"You'll be all right *if* you do what your doctor is telling you. But you won't."

She bristled. "Yes, I will."

"You didn't last time, and you won't this time. And it's not because you want anything to happen to your baby. It's just because you, who I thought could do anything, can*not* help the way you are. You won't change for anyone or anything."

Molly just sat there.

"Stress is not nothing," Adam said. "Stress killed

my father, who was the one person I knew in my life who was most like you. He was an attorney who routinely worked sixty-hour weeks. He was brilliant, driven, ambitious, like you. He never slowed down. And he had a heart attack. I was there when it happened. He died. He died because he wouldn't change, either."

"I didn't know," Molly whispered.

"No, you didn't, because I don't talk about it," Adam said. "All I do is try to live a long happy life, to be the complete opposite of him."

"The opposite of me," Molly said. "Oh, Adam."

"I wasn't the kind of man you wanted, when you thought you wanted Zach. But you weren't the kind of woman *I* wanted, not at all. Because caring for you would be risking this pain again.

"I won't," he said, "stand by and watch you do this. You were told once by the doctor about your stress and you ignored it. And you certainly never take *my* advice. I can't take the chance you won't follow through this time."

Molly stared at him, her expression crumbling.

"I'm sorry," Adam said, and swiped a hand under his eye. It came away damp. "I can't lose two more people."

He started for the curtain.

"What?" Molly asked behind him. "Where are you going?"

"Here's some cab money," he said. She didn't

reach out, so he took her hand and put the money into it. He wondered if it was the last time he'd touch her hand. The overhead florescent lighting twinkled through the diamond on her finger.

"I'll come back every few days to do some yard work and hang around," Adam said, his voice crushed as flat as his soul. "So your neighbors will see me and not suspect I'm gone. But I'm moving out. Today. I can't do this anymore."

"Adam!"

He flipped the curtain aside and stepped through, disappearing into the crowded E.R.

Chapter Twelve

Molly exited the cab, not caring that she overpaid the fare because she didn't have the energy to count the bills in her hand. Adam's car wasn't in the street, or in the driveway, and she'd so wanted it to be.

The house, her little house that was formerly happy with her as the only occupant, looked deserted already. She nearly turned and ran back up the street to the main road, where at least cars were passing by and she didn't have to be truly alone.

"Molly?" she heard, and turned to find Sylvia peering over the fence. "I was looking for you earlier, dear."

"I had to go…out," Molly answered, wishing

she'd never gone, that she'd allowed herself to relax and listen to Adam instead of bolting. He'd be here with her, smiling, cracking jokes, watching cartoons.

"Rebecca was trying to find you, also," Sylvia said. "She got a strange phone call from Rhonda. Rebecca wanted to see if you were—"

"Everything's fine," Molly lied.

"And Adam?"

"Oh—visiting his sister." Janine and the boys were staying at Adam's place, so that was less of a lie and more of an educated guess.

Sylvia appeared to want to ask more questions, but didn't. "If you need anything," she eventually said, "you don't have to look far."

"Thanks," Molly said, heading toward her front door and refusing to glance back. The sympathy on Sylvia's face was so much to bear that if Molly saw it again, she'd run back and cry on her kind neighbor's slight shoulder until she was dried out and parched.

When she entered her house, she wished she had done that. Instead, she forced herself to see the small stack of neatly folded sheets at the bottom of the stairs, and the empty spot where Elmer's water bowl had been. There was nothing else. Not even a note, which would have been something to hold in her hand, at least.

She lowered herself onto the bottom step and picked up a pillowcase, hoping and not hoping that it would smell like Adam. She held it to her nose, and the familiarity of it brought tears to her eyes.

She'd made a big, big mistake.

Adam wasn't Zach. Zach hadn't wanted to stay with her because he didn't love her.

Adam didn't want to stay with her because he *did* love her.

He did. She knew it by the way he'd said she was everything, by the way he'd rescued her sanity at the baby superstore, by the way he'd spent an entire day trying to entice her out to play. By the way he'd married her.

She rubbed at her eyes. She was going to put this right, put herself right. And she was going to do it the way she knew how.

She got up and began to hurry up the stairs, then caught herself and slowed down her pace deliberately, feeling each step creak under her foot, inhaling and exhaling on each ascent. When she got to the top, she didn't feel tired from the effort like she usually did. The breathing had rejuvenated her. She stood there and absorbed the present moment.

Then she walked just as carefully and deliberately to her office and sat down at her desk. She placed a legal pad in front of her and removed the cap from a blue pen. She poised the pen over the blank page and breathed again, five times, in and out.

Then she began her list.

"Now that you left Molly all alone—that nice, pregnant wife of yours—are you kicking us out of here?" Janine asked. She sat across from Adam at his own table, which didn't seem like his table anymore now that it was covered with drawings and math homework and a box of transparent beads that Janine made bracelets with.

"No matter how bleak things seem," Adam said, "I'm glad I can always count on my loving sibling to stand behind me."

"I'm simply saying," she went on, "that it would be extremely inconvenient."

"No, no," he said. "That's not fair to you. I'll stay with Mom."

Janine lurched up from her seat and called into the living room. "Trevor and Billy! Sit on opposite chairs! You heard me. Do *not* make me come in there." She sat back down. "Adam," she said, "I'm not really serious. The truth is I don't want you and Molly to split up. You guys are perfect for each other."

"Perfectly opposite."

"Yes," she said. "Yin and yang. Cat and dog. Uh, Cheech and Chong?"

"Quit while you're not ahead," Adam said. "It didn't work out. She's—she's like Dad."

"Who's like Dad?" he heard in the doorway. His mother, who possessed a sixth sense for when her kids were troubled, came into the room. She kissed Janine on the top of her head.

"Molly," Janine answered for her brother.

"In what way?" Pam asked, kissing Adam's

head also and sitting down between them at the round table.

"Are you kidding?" Adam asked. "You saw Dad about five minutes a week. He worked himself to— He worked too damn much. Like Molly. Her doctor says the stress is no good for her but she won't change."

"You think she'll go like your father," Pam said.

Adam didn't see the point in verbally agreeing.

"Mom!" came from the living room. "Trevor's *bothering* me!"

"It's been like this all day. Excuse me," Janine said, "while I attempt to keep my children from throttling each other."

She left, closing the door behind her.

"Molly is not your father," Pam said quietly.

"Damn nearest thing to it," Adam said.

"No," his mother insisted. "Your father didn't want to work all those hours, hon. Every night, he admitted to me that he missed us, missed spending time with you kids. But he felt he needed to bring in as much money as he could. Soon Janine was in college and you were going to be starting the year after, and my job wasn't paying much, and he worked hours and hours longer than all his colleagues so we could pay tuition without having to go without other things. I wouldn't have minded going without, but he— Your father grew up working-class, always trying to stretch his last dollar. So he wanted his own family to have so much more than we really needed. I couldn't stop him.

"He didn't love work," she said. "That's not what it was about with him. He wanted to take care of us. But it was too much for him." She looked down at the table, and Adam took her hand.

"I'm sorry, Mom. We don't even have to talk about any of this."

"We do, and it's all right. I saw the way you changed when your father left us, how you decided to take life supereasy. It suited you, so it was all right. But it doesn't suit everybody."

"Molly?"

She nodded. "I'll bet Molly's been moving since her toddler feet hit the floor. In all the time we've known her, she's been an ambitious young lady. Now, maybe at first it was to please her parents, but her parents haven't played a big part in her life for a long time. I don't think Molly works hard because of any sense of obligation to anyone. I think she works hard because she gets real, meaningful satisfaction from achievement. Would you agree?"

Adam thought about the flushed, satisfied expression Molly had when emerging from her office after a good day's work. He remembered her pride when she first showed off her decorated home and her overwhelming happiness at fighting through her fear at the baby superstore. She loved to get things done.

"Yes," he said. "But she has to change for a

little while, at least for the baby, and it's as if she doesn't know how."

"She doesn't," his mother agreed. "And having you around, most likely trying to change her entire personality from the minute you arrived at her home, probably didn't help things along. It probably made her cling more stubbornly to her old ways, so as not to let someone tell her what to do."

"Maybe, but what else could I have done?"

"Nothing really," Pam said. "You see life as you see it, and she sees it her own way. If she changes, it will have to be because she makes the decision, not because she caves to you. And if she doesn't change, you have to make your decision whether or not to live with it."

"I already left," Adam said. "I left today. I couldn't live with it. I couldn't lose her the way we lost Dad."

Pam was quiet a moment. "So you made the decision to lose her on your own terms," she said.

Adam sighed. "Yes."

"And that feels better?"

"No."

They both smiled sad smiles.

"Can I move in with you for a while?"

"I thought you'd never ask," his mother answered. "I'm hoping Molly taught you how to do laundry."

"I do laundry fine," he protested. "Maybe just not as often as you'd prefer."

"Trevor, if you don't sit down right this second,"

they heard Janine yell, "so help me, I'm going straight to jail!"

Pam chuckled. "She's a natural, your sister."

"Mom?" he asked. "How did you do it? How did you live with him, and live after him?"

"I loved him," his mother replied, "before and after. That's all."

"I suppose I'm not as brave."

"Or as old."

"You don't look a day over nineteen," he said.

His mother cupped his chin. "With charm like that, the women will be lining up outside this door again any moment."

Even if that prediction ever came true, Adam thought, the only woman he would have opened the door for would be the one woman who would stubbornly refuse to knock.

Molly shifted on the high stool at Perky Pete's, nursing a chai tea. It had taken a little self-boosting to get up there, and she didn't quite fit in the small little seat as comfortably as, say, even last month. Some time ago, she was glad to find this place, which had the armchair ambiance of a neighborhood coffeehouse but sold other drinks, as well. Molly had never considered drinking coffee, although she often wondered if she could accomplish even *more* in a day if she did.

Of course, she wasn't going to be thinking like

that anymore, starting yesterday, when she'd come home from the hospital and completed her latest list.

She slipped it out of her brown leather bag and smoothed it out on the table in front of her.

Steps To Eliminate My Stress.

It was the most important list she'd ever thought out, by far the most difficult.

And, she thought, watching her tall, blond, preppy coffee date stride in and glance around the café, she was about to cross off item number one.

She raised her hand but didn't wave it. It was a cool, professional hailing. She wasn't nervous at all. She didn't know why not.

Zach Jones warily approached her table, saw Molly a few sizes different than he'd last seen her, sighed and sat across from her. "Molly," he said.

"Zach," she answered. "I guess you've figured out what I have to tell you."

"You said on the phone it was urgent and couldn't wait. Then you said not to worry. So I figured you weren't giving me bad health news. This was the only other thing I could think of, so I'm not one hundred percent shocked, but still…"

"You didn't expect it."

"I guess I could have. But we were careful."

"I know."

Zach got up to get himself a coffee, and Molly

shook her head at his offer for a refill. She studied him while he stood at the counter, squinting at the blackboard menu. He was almost a cartoon of a fraternity boy ten years later. He wore the same sort of dark sweater, the same pressed brown khakis. His hair wasn't any thinner. It was if time had stopped around him. The only thing missing was his sparkling, handsome promise. That had crumbled into dust that Sunday afternoon, when he'd rejected her and she'd left.

She'd filled unwitting Zach with years of dreams, and now that she had emptied them out, he was just a shell, a man she used to know.

He sat down across from her with a steaming cappuccino. "What do you want to do?" he asked.

Molly waited a few seconds, but that was all he said, and he seemed to actually be expecting an answer.

"Really?" Molly asked, despite sounding rude.

"What did you think? I'd get up and walk out?"

"No, well," she amended, "more like run out screaming."

Zach smiled, but it wasn't a Zach Jones, College Dream Boy smile. It was an adult facing up to his obligations smile, and Molly was maybe more surprised to see it than he'd been surprised to learn her news.

"A few things have happened since we last met," he started.

"Tell me about it." She didn't mean to sound sarcastic, but couldn't help herself.

"I met someone," he said. "Someone really, uh, someone who—"

"Someone you fell in love with?"

He nodded.

"That's amazing."

"I think so, too," he said. "I told her about your phone call already. I told her you and I had a weekend together two months before she and I met, and I was worried this was what you might have to tell me."

"It's very admirable," Molly said, "that you were honest with her immediately."

"I can't be any other way," he said. "Not anymore, not with her." He stirred his coffee and dropped his gaze. "I'm sorry," he said, unable to look her in the eye. "I was a jerk."

"Yeah," Molly replied cheerfully. "You made me feel like crap, in fact."

"I'm not like that anymore," he said, and then he did look up. "I'm different now. I'm a changed man."

"What a coincidence," Molly said. "I'm a changed woman. Well, I'm in the process, anyway."

"I'll do whatever you want, but—"

"But you don't really want to?"

He didn't answer.

"Stick with the honesty thing," Molly urged. "It's working so far."

"No," he confessed, "in a perfect world that I controlled, I wouldn't want to. Maura and I want to have our own family." He sighed again. "That's not fair of me. In a perfect world, you wouldn't be dealing with this."

"No, guess what? I'm thrilled," Molly assured him. "By the way, I had a crush on you forever, Zach."

He had the new maturity to look embarrassed.

Molly continued, "I always thought you were going to be someone important in my future. I was close. You *provided* the important someone." She patted her belly. "And now, I'm in love with a man, too, and, well, I don't know what's going to happen with that. I do know my life is going right, and I have you to thank for part of it. I don't need you anymore."

He drew his eyebrows together. "Money?"

"No," she said. "No money, no anything. One weekend doesn't oblige you and me to each other for the rest of our lives."

Zach sat back, apparently taking in her words and turning them over in his mind. "Are you sure about this?"

"Very sure."

"Well," he said, "I'll agree, but I want to offer you one thing. Tell your child as much as you need to about us. Or don't. It's your choice. But I will always, always, be reachable. I'll notify you of my contact information every time it changes. That way, if you or the baby ever need me for money, help, anything at all, you can find me right away."

A tear slipped down Molly's face and she pressed her thumb into it, smearing it across her cheek.

"Thank you for that," she said. "And tell Maura that even though I never met her, I truly believe she must be a remarkable woman."

"She is," Zach said. "And you are, too, Molly, if I may say it."

"You may," Molly said with a grin. "After all, it's the truth."

Zach drained his cappuccino and hugged her goodbye, and when he left, the door chimes jingled behind him. She saw him hesitate on the sidewalk outside. He glanced in the window where she sat, but it was one-way glass and he must have only seen himself waving. She waved back, even though it was unnoticeable, and he turned and headed up the street, moving much more slowly than she ever remembered.

She pulled out her pen, breathed in and out, and drew a line across *1) Talk to Zach.*

As eager as she was to get to the next item on her no-stress list right away, she was forced to wait four days. Pieter Tilberg had said he wouldn't be in town until Monday.

She didn't wait by the phone for Adam to call. She wasn't foolish enough to hope he would. She did sit near the phone for much of that time, but that just happened to be because her new meditation cushion was on the floor in the living room. *"Oooooooommmmmmmmm,"* she chanted, touching her index fingers to her thumbs. Her sandalwood incense burned in the corner.

The baby kicked. “Shhh, baby,” Molly said, not opening her eyes. “No freaking out. We need to relax, relax, relax. *Oooooooommmmmmmm….*”

For four days, Molly chanted, breathed and cleared her mind of all thoughts except two—that she was missing Lou Dobbs on CNN, and that she should “om” more quietly so she could hear the phone if it happened to ring.

“Please come in, Molly,” Pieter Tilberg said, ushering her into his suite. He gestured to a chair at the executive table and they both sat. “Now, I thought we agreed I was going to contact you when I was ready to go over your recent work. You faxed your last notes to me and they were what we were looking for. Is there a problem after all?”

“No, no problem at all. Well,” she corrected herself, “there is a situation, but it has nothing to do with ALCOP. It’s a personal thing.”

Tilberg raised his brows, and that small gesture could have thwarted Molly. She’d never made this kind of statement to a client before. She wasn’t even sure she could string the words together in proper sentences.

“I’m afraid I’m having some trouble with my pregnancy,” she began. “I ended up in the hospital after several—” She stopped. Never in her life would she have admitted panic attacks, out-of-control feelings, to friends, let alone clients. She steeled herself against her misgivings and went on. "Several panic attacks, and the doctor says I need to cut down on my stress. I'm afraid that although I certainly don't want to, and I never ever expected to, I will have to change my work timetable for ALCOP."

Dreading Tilberg's response, she rushed ahead with her prepared speech. "I've drawn up a new work schedule, putting me at part-time effective just until the baby is born at the end of the year. After the baby is born, I'll work full-time. Now, I fully understand and won't be insulted if you decide that this won't be doable for you, because I promised you time I couldn't foresee that I would not be able to deliver. I can give you the names of several talented consultants with experience in human resources who I can highly recommend to take over for me. I would be willing to get them up to speed myself and..."

Tilberg held up a hand. Molly halted in the middle of a sentence, sat back and wondered if a client had ever stopped her speaking before. Usually they let her go on and on, since she was too busy wowing them to do otherwise.

"You have done a lot for us in just a couple of weeks," he began. "I hired you because you were the best candidate, and you've already exceeded my expectations. ALCOP appreciates your forthrightness with your pregnancy in the interview, as well as your honesty now. I do not want another consultant, because you have raised my standards, and I do not want to make someone else miserable trying to meet them."

He smiled. So did she.

"I think we can manage with you on a slightly slower pace for the next two months," he continued, "because I think that your slower pace is the regular pace of most anyone else I could hire."

"Probably," Molly agreed. "Good point."

"If it becomes a problem, we will talk again, but I don't expect that," Tilberg said. "A healthy baby comes first."

It occurred to her that a chauvinistic company president wouldn't exactly talk like that, but before her mind could explore it further, Tilberg said, "And how is your marriage going?"

Molly sputtered. "I don't think that's the kind of thing that you ought to be asking me," she said as delicately as she could. "It's hardly professional."

"Usually, I will agree," he said, "but in this case, I would say that this assignment and your marriage are somewhat, let's say, related?"

If Molly was still having panic attacks, this would have been the ideal moment to have one.

Instead, she sat, frozen and mute.

"Before your first interview," Tilberg said conversationally, "I had a background check done on you, which I did not have time to read. After I interviewed you and you were the top candidate, I inadvertently asked for another background check. So when I went to read them, I had two. Strangely, one said you were single, the other married. I wondered if one report was in error. I checked the date of your marriage, and discovered it was the same day as our interview."

Molly closed her eyes. This could not be happening. After all this…

"I am aware that my reputation for not hiring women to key positions precedes me," Tilberg said. "So it made me think, did one actually have to do with the other? I thought, no, it could not be."

"Mr. Tilberg—" Molly began.

He held up his hand again, and Molly fell silent again. She had no ready excuse anyway

"Now," Tilberg said, "I came up with two explanations for this extraordinary thing I found. One was that Molly Jackson would do just about anything for an opportunity she considered excellent for her career. Two was that Molly Jackson was a little bit crazy."

Molly nodded, then realizing it might seem as though she was agreeing with the latter assessment, she stilled.

"Either number one or number two," Tilberg continued, "would make you the person I want working with ALCOP. I need risk takers. You took a big, brave, insane one." He chuckled and then the chuckle turned into a laugh.

Molly began to laugh, too, and the two of them held their stomachs and clutched the side of the table. "You knew when you were at my house?" Molly managed.

"Of course," he answered, and they kept laughing until they stopped, started again, and stopped again, with some leftover guffaws escaping as they tried to resume conversation.

"I had a boss long ago," Pieter Tilberg said, "a woman, who stabbed me in the back, so to speak. Sabotaged me. I vowed never to let that happen again. I thought if I never gave another woman power, it wouldn't happen again, and I fear it's made me notoriously unfair to women ever since. And *that* is the thing I do not want to have happen again."

Molly opened her mouth to speak, but Tilberg beat her to it. "That is between you and me. I have your secret and you have mine. Agreed?"

"Agreed," Molly said. "I think you're making the right decision."

"You did, too," he replied. "I like that Adam Shibbs quite a lot. And if I am not mistaken, Ms. Consulting, he likes you a lot more than a lot. So my hope for you is that this crazy thing you have done yields more than just good things for ALCOP."

"I believe," Molly said, "it has the potential to yield something wonderful. And soon."

She stood and they shook hands. "Thank you, Mr. Tilberg," she said, "for everything."

"As you now know," he said, "I'm not a man easily

fooled. Nothing gets by me. I hope you keep that in mind for the future."

"Yes, sir," she said, serious again. She turned to go.

"Molly."

She turned back.

"Perhaps when we meet again, you can give me your recipe for those *poffertjes?*"

She struggled hard to stay solemn. "You already have one of my secrets. But I'll take it into consideration."

"Good enough."

She stepped out into the hall, closed the door behind her and muffled her laugh in her hand. She reached into her handbag and pulled out the yellow sheet of paper and her pen. She crossed out *2) Talk to Pieter Tilberg.*

Chapter Thirteen

"May I come in?"

Adam regarded Molly, standing there at his apartment door, wearing a tailored beige jacket and skirt, with tall brown boots. Despite her shape, she balanced with zero effort on two-inch heels. She held a clipboard to her chest and her briefcase dangled near her knees.

Adam smoothed a useless hand over his hair, disheveled from the sofa cushion. He went to tuck in his wrinkled T-shirt but stopped himself. Maybe it was best to stay the way he was, in case Molly needed a visual reminder of their contrasting natures.

Elmer bounded to the door and, although he

recognized Molly, he sat at Adam's feet regarding her, respectful and quiet.

Adam gestured her in, and she swept in coolly, professionally. She perched on the sofa and crossed her curvy legs at the ankle.

So much for the tearful, kissy reunion that the stupid part of him had been wanting. Even though he had been the one to leave, even though his stubbornness hadn't allowed him to contact her, his heart had been aching for Molly to come and offer him a reason to return.

He sat on the other end of the couch and waited.

"Are we alone?" she asked.

"Janine took the boys out for pizza," he said.

She didn't say anything for a few moments, and Adam had to be wrong, but she looked suspiciously like she was simply concentrating on breathing, in and out, five times. Then she spoke again. "We had an agreement," she started, "and you're not carrying out your end of the bargain."

Her voice was neutral, but her gaze was unable to settle on him, instead darting around the room. It was only a tiny hint, but enough of one that Adam resolved to hear her out.

"That's right," he answered, giving her nothing in return until he worked out what her goal here was.

"And due to unforeseen circumstances, I have come to the realization that our terms really can't stand. We're going to have to agree on a new plan."

Adam's heart sank as far down as he feared it would eventually go when he married Molly Jackson.

"I have here," she said, "a new proposal, which I have drawn up. I'll give you a summary of the major points, if that's all right."

Adam nodded, his whole body weary.

"I'm proposing that we scrap the original term of one year and write the new term in as indefinite, up to and not a day less than forever."

Adam dared to look at her. She consulted her notes.

"In addition," she said, "you will continue to reside full-time in the home at Seven Danbury Way, but you will no longer be permitted your own sleeping accommodations. You will instead share whatever bed I will be sleeping in myself."

A smile lurked in the corners of Adam's mouth.

"Also," Molly said, "you will continue to observe, without fail, September eighth of every year as our official anniversary, with appropriate activity and celebration. Failure to recall such date each year will relegate you to temporarily modified sleeping accommodations, which most likely will involve Elmer."

Adam's smile cracked open wide, even though Molly's face remained granite.

"You will teach the baby, beginning at the yet-to-be-determined exact date it enters the world, to relax and have fun every day, to strive for greatness while at the same time enjoying all life has to offer. Homework assistance, Barbie fashion shows and

Little League could be factors. You will likely be called upon to answer to the name of Dad, Daddy, or variations on the theme.

"Speaking of name," she continued, "I agree to make a permanent alteration in that category, mainly because Ms. Consulting will look great on business cards."

She abruptly tossed her clipboard to the floor, where it landed with a clatter. She pulled open her briefcase and opened it. It was empty, except for one piece of lined yellow paper, folded over once. She pulled it out and held it in her hand. Then she met Adam's gaze head-on, staring fearless into his eyes.

"You were not for me," she said, dropping her professional tone, "and I was not for you. But that was before. Now we're right. Because *you* were right. I needed to change."

"Not completely," he interrupted. "Not who you are. I was wrong to try to make you morph into the female me."

"True," she conceded, "but certain things in life do require a flexibility I didn't realize I was capable of. After this baby is born, I intend to work just as hard as I always did, but I will keep alert for the approaching moments where I need to adjust, and allow myself to enjoy what I'm lucky enough to have. You won't have to stand by and watch me self-destruct. It won't happen."

She held up the paper. "This was my plan for the week. My no-stress action plan. I told Zach about the baby, and we came to amicable agreement that he wouldn't be in my future. I talked to Tilberg, and informed him I'd be cutting down my work load for the rest of the year."

She unfolded the paper. "You're last on the list because I had to square away the other things first. But you're the most important item. The most stressful thing in my life in the last month has been refusing to admit to you and to myself that I've fallen in love with you. I said it the day I went to the hospital, but I could have, should have said it long before that."

"I should have said at the reunion that I'm in love with you," Adam said.

"I should have said it in college."

"What?" Adam laughed out loud. "You wouldn't have said it in college if your life—no, if your *grades*—depended on it."

"Maybe I would have if you weren't such a pain in the butt."

"*I* was not the pain in the butt."

She stopped. "Come home," she said, her eyes shining. "Between the two of us, we know how to build a successful, satisfying, happy, long future."

They collided into each other on the middle of the sofa, a tangle of skin and kisses, tears coming from someone and ending up on the other's face. Elmer leaped onto their pile, shivering with joy.

After several happy minutes, Adam reluctantly released her and reached for the cordless phone.

"Who are you calling?" Molly asked. "I know, a supermarket tabloid to tip them on our unlikely romance. Although maybe it's not as interesting as aliens taking over Caesar's Palace."

"Good idea, but no," Adam said. "I'm calling Janine's cell phone. Don't you think she and the boys deserve a nice night out? I'll strongly suggest she take them to a movie. Preferably a double-feature."

He lifted Molly's hand to his lips and kissed it, her diamond ring poking his top lip. "We have some deal sealing to take care of here," he said, "and I don't want to be interrupted."

He stopped and sniffed at the cuff of her crisp white shirt. "Um, I smell incense."

She blushed a becoming rosy pink. "Sorry," she began, but he threw back his head and laughed.

"Don't be sorry," he said. "I like it."

"Oddly enough, so do I," she replied, then smiled. "It smells like comfort. It smells like…home."

* * * * *

What happens when workaholic attorney
Jack Lever hires free-spirited Zooey Finnegan
to be a nanny for his two children?
Find out in the next installment in the
TALK OF THE NEIGHBORHOOD *continuity,*
MOTHER-IN-TRAINING
by reader favorite Marie Ferrarrella.
On sale October 2006
wherever Silhouette Books are sold.

Set in darkness beyond the ordinary world.
Passionate tales of life and death.
With characters' lives ruled by laws the everyday world can't begin to imagine.

Introducing NOCTURNE, a spine-tingling new line from Silhouette Books.

The thrills and chills begin with UNFORGIVEN by Lindsay McKenna

Plucked from the depths of hell, former military sharpshooter Reno Manchahi was hired by the government to kill a thief, but he had a mission of his own. Descended from a family of shape-shifters, Reno vowed to get the revenge he'd thirsted for all these years. But his mission went awry when his target turned out to be a powerful seductress, Magdalena Calen Hernandez, who risked everything to battle a potent evil. Suddenly, Reno had to transform himself into a true hero and fight the enemy that threatened them all. He had to become a Warrior for the Light....

Turn the page for a sneak preview of UNFORGIVEN by Lindsay McKenna. On sale September 26, wherever books are sold.

Chapter 1

One shot...one kill.

The sixteen-pound sledgehammer came down with such fierce power that the granite boulder shattered instantly. A spray of glittering mica exploded into the air and sparkled momentarily around the man who wielded the tool as if it were a weapon. Sweat ran in rivulets down Reno Manchahi's drawn, intense face. Naked from the waist up, the hot July sun beating down on his back, he hefted the sledgehammer skyward once more. Muscles in his thick forearms leaped and biceps bulged. Even his breath was focused on the boulder. In his mind's eye, he pictured Army General Robert Hampton's fleshy, arrogant fifty-year-old features on the rock's surface. Air exploded from between his lips as he brought the avenging hammer down. The boulder pulverized beneath his funneled hatred.

One shot...one kill...

Nostrils flaring, he inhaled the dank, humid heat and drew it deep into his massive lungs. Revenge allowed Reno to endure his imprisonment at a U.S. Navy brig near San Diego, California. Drops of sweat were flung in all directions as the crack of his sledgehammer claimed a third stone victim. Mouth taut, Reno moved to the next boulder.

The other prisoners in the stone yard gave him a wide berth. They always did. They instinctively felt his simmering hatred, the palpable revenge in his cinnamon-colored eyes, was more than skin-deep.

And they whispered he was different.

Reno enjoyed being a loner for good reason. He came from a medicine family of shape-shifters. But even this secret power had not protected him—or his family. His wife, Ilona, and his three-year-old daughter, Sarah, were dead. Murdered by Army General Hampton in their former home on USMC base in Camp Pendleton, California. Bitterness thrummed through Reno as he savagely pushed the toe of his scarred leather boot against several smaller pieces of gray granite that were in his way.

The sun beat down upon Manchahi's naked shoulders, grown dark red over time, shouting his half-

Apache heritage. With his straight black hair grazing his thick shoulders, copper skin and broad face with high cheekbones, everyone knew he was Indian. When he'd first arrived at the brig, some of the prisoners taunted him and called him Geronimo. Something strange happened to Reno during his fight with the name-calling prisoners. Leaning down after he'd won the scuffle, he'd snarled into each of their bloodied faces that if they were going to call him anything, they would call him *gan,* which was the Apache word for *devil.*

His attackers had been shocked by the wounds on their faces, the deep claw marks. Reno recalled doubling his fist as they'd attacked him en masse. In that split second, he'd gone into an altered state of consciousness. In times of danger, he transformed into a jaguar. A deep, growling sound had emitted from his throat as he defended himself in the three-against-one fracas. It all happened so fast that he thought he had imagined it. He'd seen his hands morph into a forearm and paw, claws extended. The slashes left on the three men's faces after the fight told him he'd begun to shape-shift. A fist made bruises and swelling; not four perfect, deep claw marks. Stunned and anxious, he hid the knowledge of what else he was from these prisoners. Reno's only defense was to make all the prisoners so damned scared of him and remain a loner.

Alone. Yeah, he was alone, all right. The steel hammer swept downward with hellish ferocity. As the granite groaned in protest, Reno shut his eyes for just a moment. Sweat dripped off his nose and square chin.

Straightening, he wiped his furrowed, wet brow and looked into the pale blue sky. What got his attention was the startling cry of a red-tailed hawk as it flew over the brig yard. Squinting, he watched the bird. Reno could make out the rust-colored tail on the hawk. As a kid growing up on the Apache reservation in Arizona, Reno knew that all animals that appeared before him were messengers.

Brother, what message do you bring me? Reno knew one had to ask in order to receive. Allowing the sledgehammer to drop to his side, he concentrated on the hawk who wheeled in tightening circles above him.

Freedom! the hawk cried in return.

Reno shook his head, his black hair moving against his broad, thickset shoulders. *Freedom? No way, Brother. No way.* Figuring that he was making up the hawk's shrill message, Reno turned away. Back to his rocks. Back to picturing Hampton's smug face.

Freedom!

* * * * *

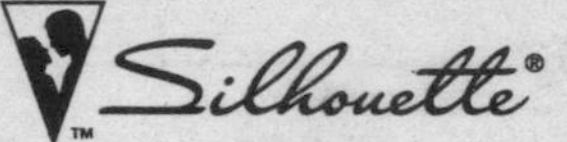

SPECIAL EDITION®

COMING NEXT MONTH

#1783 IT TAKES A FAMILY—Victoria Pade
Northbridge Nuptials
Penniless and raising an infant niece after her sister's death, Karis Pratt's only hope was to go to Northbridge, Montana, and find the baby's father, Luke Walker. Did this small-town cop hold the key to renewed family ties and a bright new future for Karis?

#1784 ROCK-A-BYE RANCHER—Judy Duarte
When rugged Clay Callaghan asked attorney Dani De La Cruz to help bring his orphaned granddaughter back from Mexico, Dani couldn't say no to the case…but what would she say to the smitten cattleman's more personal proposals?

#1785 MOTHER IN TRAINING—Marie Ferrarella
Talk of the Neighborhood
When Zooey Finnegan walked out on her fiancé, the gossips pounced. Unfazed, she went on to work wonders as nanny to widower Jack Lever's two kids. But when she got Jack to come out of his own emotional shell...the town *really* had something to talk about!

#1786 UNDER HIS SPELL—Kristin Hardy
Holiday Hearts
Lainie Trask's longtime crush on J. J. Cooper hadn't amounted to much—J.J. seemed too busy with World Cup skiing and womanizing to notice the feisty curator. But an injury led to big changes for J.J.—including plenty of downtime to discover Lainie's charms….

#1787 LOVE LESSONS—Gina Wilkins
Medical researcher Dr. Catherine Travis had all the trappings of the good life…except for someone special to share it with. Would maintenance man and part-time college student Mike Clancy fix what ailed the good doctor…despite the odds arrayed against them?

#1788 NOT YOUR AVERAGE COWBOY—
Christine Wenger
When rancher Buck Porter invited famous cookbook author and city slicker Merry Turner to help give Rattlesnake Ranch a makeover, it was a recipe for trouble. So what was the secret ingredient that soon made the cowboy, his young daughter and Merry inseparable?

SSECNM0906